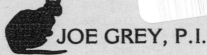 **JOE GREY, P.I.**

"Go home!" Joe yelled.

The effect was memorable. The dogs stopped barking and jerked to attention—then started looking around frantically for humans.

"Get out! Get the hell away!"

They stared at Joe, then backed away, their ears and tails low, lips pulled back in smiles of fear.

"Go on, you mangy retards. Get yourselves home!"

They turned as one and ran off in a pack, careening down the hill.

Joe Grey smiled, licked his whiskers and stretched. Whatever the source of his unusual talent, it had its up side.

Cat
on the
Edge

Shirley Rousseau Murphy

AVON BOOKS
An Imprint of HarperCollinsPublishers

This is a work of fiction. Names, characters, places, and incidents are products of the author's imagination or are used fictitiously and are not to be construed as real. Any resemblance to actual events, locales, organizations, or persons, living or dead, is entirely coincidental.

AVON BOOKS
An Imprint of HarperCollins*Publishers*
10 East 53rd Street
New York, New York 10022-5299

First Avon Books printing: April 2000
First HarperPrism printing: June 1996

Avon Trademark Reg. U.S. Pat. Off. and in Other Countries, Marca Registrada, Hecho en U.S.A.
HarperCollins® is a trademark of HarperCollins Publishers Inc.

Printed in the U.S.A.

10 9

For those who wonder about their cats. And for the cats who don't need to wonder, for the cats who know.

Cat on the
Edge

1

The murder of Samuel Beckwhite in the alley behind Jolly's Delicatessen was observed by no human witness. Only the gray tomcat saw Beckwhite fall, the big man's heavy body crumpling, his round, close-trimmed head crushed from the blow of a shiny steel wrench. At the bright swing of the weapon and the thud of breaking bone, the cat stiffened with alarm and backed deeper into the shadows, a sleek silver ripple in the dark.

The attack on Beckwhite came without warning. The two men entered the brick-paved alley, walking side by side beneath the dim light of a decorative lamp affixed to the brick wall beside the window of a small shop. The men were talking softly, in a friendly manner. The cat looked up at them carelessly from beside the concealed garbage can, where he was feasting on smoked salmon. The men exchanged no harsh word; Joe caught no scent of anger or distress before the smaller man struck Beckwhite.

Though the evening sky was already dark, the shops along the alley were still open, their doors softly lit by the two wrought-iron wall sconces, one at either end of the short lane. The stained glass door of the tiny tearoom reflected the lamplight in round, gleaming patterns of blue and red. The narrow, leaded glass doors leading to the antique shop and the art gallery glinted with interior lights warped into circular designs against the darkness. The closed door to the bistro presented a solid blue face, but there were lights within behind its small, leaded windows, and the easy beat of a forties love song could be heard. The golf shop lights reflected out around the edges of its half-closed shutters, and the shopkeeper could be glimpsed deep within, toting up figures, preparing to close up and go home. The soft thud of the wrench could not have reached him; he did not look up. There was no sound from the alley to alert anyone to the murder which had just occurred within that peaceful lane.

Between each pair of shop doors stood a large ceramic pot planted with a flowering oleander tree. The pink-and-white blossoms shone waxen in the dim light. All Molena Point's alleys were small, inviting oases designed to welcome both villagers and tourists. At the near end of the lane, where the tomcat was eating, one ordinary, unremarkable wooden door shut away the kitchen of the delicatessen. The busy front door was around the corner. The trellis, and the sweet-scented jasmine vine which climbed it, concealed behind its lower foliage the delicatessen's two garbage cans, and now concealed, as well, the astonished cat.

Here in the alley, Jolly's employees received

deliveries and brought out their discreetly wrapped trash to discard, carefully saving back the nicest delicacies, which they put down on soggy paper plates for the village cats.

The cats of Molena Point were not strays—most were blessed with comfortable homes—but every cat in the village knew Jolly's and partook greedily of its rich offerings of leftover broiled chicken, pastrami, a spoonful of salmon salad from an abandoned plate, a sliver of brie or Camembert, or the scraps from a roast beef sandwich from which mustard must be scraped away with a fastidious paw. Joe ate well at home, sharing his master's supper, but Jolly's menu ran more to his tastes and less to fried onions, fried potatoes, and hamburger, and he had only to chase off an occasional contender. He had, at this time in his life, no aversion to eating after humans. And he liked George Jolly; the soft, round old man in his white clothes and white apron would come out sometimes and watch the cats eating, and smile and talk to them. If George Jolly had been in the alley at that moment, the murder very likely would not have occurred. The two men would have walked on through. Though the killer might simply have waited for his next opportunity; it was not a crime of sudden passion.

There was nothing Joe could have done to prevent Beckwhite's murder even if he had so desired, the action coming down too fast. As the men talked softly, strolling along, the shorter man, with no change of tone or expression, no shifting of pace, suddenly produced the chrome wrench in a whirl of motion describing a bright arc. His swinging weapon hit Beckwhite so hard that Joe heard Beckwhite's skull crack. Beckwhite collapsed to the brick paving, limp as an empty rat skin.

At the far end of the alley, behind the last oleander tree, a shadow moved, then was still, or was gone, impossible to know; but neither the killer nor the crouching tomcat saw it—their attention was on the deed at hand.

No question that the victim was dead or swiftly dying. Joe could sense his death, could smell it. The sharp grip of death shivered through him like a sudden winter chill.

Joe knew who the dead man was. Samuel Beckwhite owned the local auto agency, and he was Joe's master's business associate, the two shared a large, handsome establishment at the upper end of the village. Joe had at first supposed the other man was a customer for one of Beckwhite's mint condition BMWs or Mercedeses, or maybe he worked for Beckwhite and the two were taking a shortcut back to the car agency. He found the smaller man offensive, his walk unnaturally silent, his voice and accent too soft, too artful.

But then, there weren't that many humans Joe liked, nothing to cause alarm; until he saw the bright wrench swing up. Swiftly the deed was done. Beckwhite fell and lay still. The damp breath of the sea and of eucalyptus trees scented the alley, mixed with the perfume of the jasmine vines. Above the love song's soft, nostalgic melody an occasional hush of tires could be heard on some nearby street;

and Joe could hear the sea crashing six blocks away, against the rocky cliffs. The evening had turned chill.

Behind Joe, beyond the alley, the small seaside village was quiet and unheeding. It was a charming, unpretentious town, its shops sheltered by broad old oak trees. The shops mingled easily among a few bed-and-breakfast establishments and private cottages and between the newer, larger structures of the library, and of the courthouse and police station. Many of the stores and galleries, in fact, occupied remodeled cottages dating from a time when Molena Point was a mere speck on the map, a tiny seaside retreat. Now its residential area climbed the hills crowding ever higher up into California's dry, rugged coastal range.

And the lights scattered across the hills picked out the half-hidden rooftops of new homes among the masses of pines and oaks. The larger homes were downplayed, well hidden among the trees. The population of Molena Point was divided between artists and writers, tourists, and a handful of famous names, many of whom were connected with the film industry centered 350 miles south; though Molena Point itself had little in common with Hollywood. It was a slow, easy environ, where doors were often left unlocked, and violent crime was uncommon.

At the moment of the murder, the tomcat was aware of no traffic on the two adjoining streets, and no foot traffic on the sidewalks which passed the alley. Across the herringbone-patterned brick the body was not touched by lamplight, but lay in a deep patch of darkness, shadowed by an oleander tree and by a jutting wall. During the murder and directly afterward no one entered any shop door and no one left. Only Joe saw the killer: he was a thin, stooped man, maybe five-ten, though it was hard to tell a human's height from Joe's low vantage point. He was round-shouldered, and dressed in a plain, dark sweatshirt, dark jeans, and dark running shoes. He stood looking down at his victim, then suddenly looked up, straight at Joe.

He looked puzzled.

Staring at the cat, his expression shifted to startled recognition, then to cold fear.

And suddenly rage sliced across his face and he lunged at Joe, swinging his weapon.

Joe spun around, but the trellis blocked his escape. Hissing, he backed along the wall of the building until his rear pressed against the door to the delicatessen. But now he was blocked by a large, potted tree. When the killer swung the metal bar he dodged again, feinting and ducking, praying the door behind him would open, praying to escape inside the deli among friendly, white-trousered legs.

The door remained closed. And the man stood straddle-legged before him weaving and dodging, blocking his escape. Joe's fear turned him cold and weak. The man lunged to grab him, and Joe struck out fiercely, but his claws missed the thin, pale face. The killer lunged again and snatched at him, and his hands were on him. Joe clawed and fought, felt flesh tear, and he twisted away and dived between the garbage cans and the wall.

The man closed in, swinging the wrench. Joe leaped over the cans and over his flashing arm and fled from the alley to the street, streaking across the sidewalk and into the street directly in front of a cruising police car. Brakes squealed. He twisted and leaped away to safety beneath a parked car.

He crouched in blackness beside a tire that reeked of dog pee, and stared out at the street, where the police had pulled to a stop.

The officers shone a flashlight beam into the alley, its moving glow flashing eerily across potted trees and jutting doorways; but the light did not reach deep enough to pick out the murdered man. Beckwhite's dark-suited body lay indistinguishable from the shadows, his white shirt seeming no more than a twist of discarded newspaper.

Beyond Beckwhite, against a dark wall, the killer stood frozen, his face averted and hidden by his lank hair, his own dark clothing blending with the brick.

The police, expecting no trouble in the quiet village, doused their flashlights and moved on, perhaps laughing at the cat that had run through their headlights, nearly getting himself creamed.

The instant they had gone the killer was after him. The man knelt to look under the car, then circled it as if to drive him out. In a minute he'd kneel again, and reach under.

Joe thought about it for only a second. He could stay here, dodging back and forth under the car as the thin man circled him; or he could run.

He fled. If this man would kill a human, he wouldn't hesitate to knock off a cat.

The question was, why? He was only a cat. What did the man think? That he would run to the police with what he had seen? But, racing away through the dark streets, fleeing for his life, he didn't wonder long; he concentrated on the problem at hand. In this block there was nowhere to hide—the shops were joined tight together. There was no escape between. The man's footsteps thundered behind him: he was fast, dodging and swerving as Joe swerved.

Panicked, Joe slid around the corner and dived under a wooden porch, the first shelter he could think of, and through a hole in the foundation.

He knew the house well; he had a sometime lady love here. The old house had found new life as an antique shop. The dark earth underneath, in the low crawl space, was cold beneath his paws and smelled sour, heavy with mildew and cat pee.

As he raced away from the hole, cobwebs hanging from the sagging floor timbers clung to his ears and whiskers. He felt them pull away, sticky and clinging. He sped through, dodging the furnace and the gas and water pipes and hanging electrical wires, toward an opening at the back.

Before he burst out into the backyard he turned to look behind him.

The small rectangular hole he had come through was blocked. No light shone in from the street, only the dark bulk of the killer reaching in, his arm and shoulder filling the little space. Joe could hear scraping as if he was trying to climb through.

So come on, buster. Crawl on in here. Get yourself trapped under these timbers and pipes, so I can rake you good.

But on second thought, he fled. *Why push it? Get the hell away from the guy.*

Only faintly ashamed at his cowardice he streaked away, out through the hole at the back into the antique shop's backyard. He heard the man running, coming around through the side yard.

The small, scruffy backyard was empty. Bolting for the sidewalk, he careened along the side street, his ears twitching back, listening behind him. When he heard the man running, he swarmed up a rose trellis that climbed the wall of Julia's French Pancakes, onto the sloped shingled roof.

He could hear, below, the killer coming along the sidewalk. He crouched at the edge, looking down, trying to keep his weight off the rusty roof gutter.

The dark figure was searching for him under a line of azalea bushes growing in the parking strip between the sidewalk and the street. Joe backed away from the edge and trotted away over the rooftops.

Over Julia's, then across the top of the bookstore, then the Nugent Gallery and across the roof of an import place that always smelled of straw and spices—though its roof smelled only of tar. At the end of the row, at another side street, he dropped onto the thick limb of an oak so old and huge that the sidewalk had been built to curve around it, dangerously narrowing the street at that point. The tree covered the entire street to the other side, and was a favorite aerial crossing for the village cats. He'd had some pleasant rendezvous there.

He crossed the street within the branches and leaped up to the next line of roofs. Trotting to the end, listening, he heard only silence now. No running footsteps, only the hush of a lone car passing.

When he was certain the killer had gone he came down warily from the roof of Molena Point Cleaners, clinging among a bougainvillea vine. Dropping to the ground, he galloped two blocks east, then turned back south in the direction of home. Zigzagging through a dozen backyards and across two streets, he could hear nothing following now.

But fear still clutched at his belly, fear not of the immediate pursuit—he'd lost the guy—but fear of an even more frightening nature. Fear of something far more terrifying than being chased through the night-dark streets by a man swinging a wrench; though in fact, his last glimpse of the killer had shown him no weapon; probably the guy had dropped it in his pocket, against the moment it would be needed to smash one small tomcat.

Just before he reached Ocean Avenue, which divided the village with its wide, tree-shaded median, he swarmed up into the high, concealing branches of a eucalyptus that hung over the ice-cream shop. If the killer was following, walking softly, Joe didn't want to lead him right to his own house.

He crouched among the foliage trying to understand what was happening. Why had the killer chased him? He was only a cat. Why would the man think a cat could tell anyone who had killed Beckwhite?

Though the fact was, Joe could easily finger the killer. He could, in fact, in any number of creative ways, give the police a detailed description of the man.

But the killer could not know this. No way could he know. How could the thin, hunched man know that he, Joe Grey, could bear witness to the murder?

He sat shivering on the branches, so upset he didn't even wash.

And he was not only scared and puzzled, but his mind was filled with other strange thoughts, as well. With decidedly disturbing and uncatlike responses to the immediate events.

For one thing, besides fear for his own gray hide, of which he was very fond, he was feeling remorse for the dead man. And that was unfeline and stupid.

Why should he care that Beckwhite was dead? He hadn't even known the man. It was hypocrisy of the highest degree to pretend that he felt sorry for Samuel Beckwhite.

But yet he did feel sorry, a dark little cloud of mourning hovered over him, sentimental and totally without basis. He felt sick at the brutality of the premeditated killing.

The murder he had witnessed had been twisted and sick. It had nothing in common with the way a cat killed.

Cats killed for food or to keep their skills honed. Mother cats killed to teach their young to hunt. Cats did not kill with the cold deliberation he had just witnessed. That thin, tunnel-eyed man had killed as casually as if he were culminating a financial transaction—paying his lunch bill or buying a newspaper. And it was Joe's very analysis of the event that alarmed him.

He backed down from the tree and headed home thinking heavy thoughts; crossing the grassy median then padding along the dark sidewalk warily watching the shadows, his whole being was tainted with a philosophical distress belonging, rightfully, only to humans.

Perusal of the human mind was not a feline concern. Cats didn't *think* about human perversion. Cats *felt* human depravity. They knew that human lust and dark human hatred existed, and they accepted those aberrations. Cats did not analyze those warped human conditions. Cats left the philosophizing to men.

Yet all the time he had been fleeing from the killer, a part of him had been trying to analyze the man. Trying to guess at the man's motives. Trying to figure out his intentions not only at chasing him, but his purpose in killing Beckwhite. Trying to unravel the mystery that had transformed that thin human face into a killer's mask.

What did he care what drove the man to kill? He wasn't connected to this man's problem, and he didn't want to be. And inside him, alarms were going off. These thoughts were new and terrifying. A gut level signal was warning him that he was in the throes of mental and emotional change. A new facet of himself had awakened, new concerns were surfacing.

The transformation had been coming on him for some weeks, but it had not been stirred violently alive, not until tonight. Now, some foreign presence within him had come alert. And it was clawing to get out, to break free.

He ran the last two blocks caught in a distressing tangle of fears and wanting nothing more complicated than his warm, safe bed, wanted to curl up safe on the blanket next to Clyde, protected by his human housemate.

2

The gray cat woke suddenly from deep sleep, curled on his master's bed. Something had waked him, a noise foreign to the usual house noises. He twitched an ear, trying to come alert.

The violent screeching came again, jerking him up to full attention, propelling him to his feet, his claws digging into the blanket, his senses slapped into high gear by the splintering, wrenching sound. *What the hell is going on?* Ears flattened, his stub tail tucked low, he stared around the dim bedroom, a growl rumbling deep in his throat. The splintering cacophony had driven every hair along his spine straight up, stiff as the bristles on a hairbrush. Standing rigid on the double bed next to his human companion, he tried to get a fix on the sound.

Beside him, Clyde turned over, heat radiating from his body like a furnace. His snores rose a decibel, to effectively drown the next scraping of metal on wood.

That's what the sound was, metal on wood. As if a window were being pried open. Joe sniffed the chill air, trying to scent the intruder, but Clyde's breath was such a powerful decoction of red wine and raw onions that he couldn't have smelled a convention of sweaty joggers if they had crowded into the bedroom. He moved away from Clyde's warm shoulder, listening intently. He wasn't sure whether the noise had come from right there in the room or from another part of the house.

He felt outrage that a burglar would bother them. This was a small, peaceful village, and a quiet street. They had never had a break-in, not since they'd moved there. This wasn't, after all, the mean streets of south San Francisco. But at contemplation of an invader in the house, a cold fear held him, far more chilling than wariness of a normal burglar.

Shivering and puzzled, he studied the dim bedroom, the hulking shapes of dresser, of the TV, of Clyde's clothes flung over the chair limp as a used Halloween costume discarded after the big event. Clyde's shoes protruded from the shadow beneath the chair, and beside them one smelly sock.

Nothing seemed unfamiliar in the bedroom. Warily Joe crept across the covers and hunched over the side of the bed, staring under.

The shadows beneath the bedsprings were empty, nothing there but a few dust balls like the ghosts of long-deceased mice. He backed up onto the bed again and licked a paw, scanning the room's corners, its darkest reaches, staring into the open closet, at the dim tangle of Clyde's clothes.

No shadow seemed unaccounted for. On the dark bedroom walls, three pale rectangles shone, the mirror gleaming silver, the two window shades gathering artificial light from without, from the streetlamp up at the corner. And the dim glow of the shades was struck across with the shadows of twisted branches, from the oak tree that sheltered the bedroom. Suddenly, within the tree, a mockingbird began to babble, its tuneless gurgles blending with Clyde's snores.

He could hear nothing, now, but snores and the damned bird. What was it with mockingbirds? What went through their tiny minds? The creature was as tuneless as a baboon practicing the violin.

But the mockingbird wouldn't be sitting in that tree trying to sing, if someone were out there under the bedroom windows.

Maybe the scraping noise had come from the backyard. Or maybe from the front of the house; maybe up beyond the front porch a stranger hugged the perimeter of the house, trying to force his way in, to pry open a living room window, or the front door.

Joe leaped to the floor, the shock of his weight keening through his soft pads and up his legs, jolting the muscles of his shoulders.

He was a big cat, heavy, his silver-gray coat gleaming dense and short, sleek as gray velvet over hard muscle. Tense, flattening his ears and whiskers tight to his head, he prowled the room, listening through the walls. Moving through the dark room, his gray parts blended into the shadows so the white marks on his chest and paws and the white triangle on his nose seemed to move disconnected.

He was not a handsome cat. The strip of white

down his nose made his yellow eyes seem too close together, gave him a permanent frown.

The splintering, wrenching noise did not come again. Could he have dreamed that sound, only imagined it?

Certainly he had imagined some strange things lately, so strange that he had begun to think some feline disease was slowly rotting his brain.

Maybe he'd had a nightmare caused by bad food. That had happened once when he got hold of a sick gopher; he'd had wild, impossible dreams.

He tried to remember what he had eaten yesterday. He'd had a hasty mouse after supper, but that shouldn't do it, he'd eaten it an hour after his usual cat food. If it was going to make him sick, it would have done so long before now. Anyway, the mouse had gone down delightfully. He'd killed a starling around noon yesterday, but he'd spit out the beak and feet. Starlings never made him sick. Preoccupied with his physical assessment, he didn't realize he was keening deep in his throat until Clyde woke, swearing.

"For Christ sake, Joe, stop it! It's too damned early to be horny! Go back to sleep!" Only then was Joe aware of his own harsh, rough-edged crying.

Silenced, he listened again for the dry, quick report of breaking wood. He really should check the house. The dogs couldn't do it, they were shut in the kitchen. The two old dogs had spent their nights in the kitchen ever since Barney started peeing on the front door. And both dogs slept like rocks, lifeless as the products of a taxidermist's art. Someone was breaking into the house and the damned dogs hadn't the presence of mind to wake up and bark. Both were big dogs, a scruffy golden and an overweight Lab, both could have routed a prowler with their barking alone if they'd made half an effort.

Absently he licked a whisker. He considered himself the epitome of tough tomcats, yet now he felt strangely reluctant to leave the safety of the bedroom. Shivers of fear coursed up his rigid back, and his paws had begun to sweat.

Trying to get hold of himself, he cocked an ear toward the closed door. Hearing no creak in the hall, he approached the door warily, and pawed it open. Crouching, he slunk down the dark hall, his whiskers tingling with apprehension.

He stared into the bathroom, looking nervously past the shower door into the tiled cubicle. When he found it empty, he slipped on down the hall along the dog-scented carpet toward the spare bedroom.

That room was at the back, without the streetlight to brighten its interior. The shades were up. He could see no movement beyond the black glass. He jumped on the desk, pressed his face against a cold pane of glass, and looked out.

He could see no one in the backyard. He could hear no sound, now, from anywhere in the house. Yet still he could not stop his skin from rippling in long, chilling shivers.

Terror had plagued him ever since that night in the alley when he saw Samuel Beckwhite murdered. He could not escape these constant replays of that bright arc swinging up, the dull thud of shattering bone. That moment of violence had altered his every thought, his every reaction. Sometimes he wondered if he was going bonkers, tipping over the edge. And it was far more than his witness to Beckwhite's death, and his subsequent pursuit, that had transformed him.

The weirdness started before that. He was, and had been for some weeks, experiencing a strange identity change. He was totally out of touch with the normal cat world. His initial amazement when he realized he could understand human speech had been almost more than he could handle.

Nothing that life could serve up could equal the shock of that first moment when human speech became clear. When Clyde said in a low, controlled voice, "If you don't take that mouse outside, Joe, you are going to find yourself warming a cat coffin with the lid nailed down."

He had understood each individual word. He had taken the mouse outdoors, so upset at his sudden cognitive ability that he turned the squirming morsel loose, let it go free to scamper away.

He had stood on the porch shivering with astonishment at his sudden understanding of human speech.

A normal, ordinary cat knows the call to meals, he knows and tolerates his master's sharp commands such as *Get off the table!* and *Stop that damned clawing!* Any cat with a home knows the love words, the baby talk. But words such as those are recognized partly through tone of voice, partly through frequent repetition. No cat is able to decode every human word, or to comprehend abstract human meaning.

But he, Joe Grey, was able to do exactly that. Was suddenly able to absorb each subtle implication, to sort out all the intricacies of human innuendo. From that moment, when Clyde shouted at him about the mouse, he had understood every word between Clyde and his poker-playing buddies or his girlfriends; he was highly amused by Clyde's tangled telephone conversations when he tried to keep each woman ignorant of his involvement with the others. Though he didn't know what women saw in Clyde.

Clyde Damen was thirty-eight, of medium height, with straight black hair and thick shoulders. He had been married once, but he didn't talk about it. Joe hadn't known him then. Clyde had no great beauty or charm that Joe could see, yet there were always women cooking dinner for him, bringing over steaks or casseroles, snuggling up on the couch with the lights low and a CD playing something soft and throbbing.

Since Joe began to understand every intimate word between Clyde and his lady friends, their visits had been both embarrassing and boring. Usually, he left the house.

Human speech would be fine if it did not run to such crass inanities. For instance, he understood the TV news, knew the economy was in bad shape, knew that the president had recalled his ambassadors to half a dozen Eastern countries, but why all the fuss? The basic moves were little different than the eternal manipulations of two tomcats, or of cat and mouse. So what was the big deal? Did they have to go on about it? Well, maybe he didn't have the right frame of reference.

And in the daytime, prowling the bushes or sleeping in the neighbors' flower beds, every pair of gossiping housewives pelted his brain with unwanted gossip and inane opinions. And the neighborhood men, working on their cars or digging crabgrass were just as annoying. These conversations were no longer just noise; now he was a suddenly a captive audience, drawn to paying unwilling attention. The human world had, in short, intruded into his world, distracting him from hunting and frustrating his leisure hours with trivia.

Face it, he was no longer a normal cat, his time divided between satisfying bouts of fighting, mating, eating, sleeping, and bullying his housemates, both feline and canine, and bullying Clyde. He was jumpy and off his feed; he had lost all heart for bullying and almost for lovemaking.

Beyond the spare room windows, out in the dark backyard, nothing moved. And the room itself could conceal no one—it held only the seldom-used guest bed with boxes of canned dog food underneath, and Clyde's weight lifting equipment and his messy desk.

He moved away from the distressing scene of Clyde's bachelor decor and crept on down the hall to the dining alcove, passing the kitchen door. Surely the dogs would wake if someone were breaking into the kitchen. Or at least the three other cats would wake and make a fuss, subsequently waking the dogs. Then, heading for the living room, he heard the scraping again.

It was coming from the front windows. Someone was outside the windows trying to get inside. Enraged, forgetting fear, he crept across the worn faux-Persian rug, keeping low, stalking the sound. The shades were up, the draperies open—Clyde seldom bothered to pull them unless he had female guests.

Beyond the windows, dawn was beginning to touch the night sky, its first thin light seeping down between pale clouds. He leaped to the sill, to look out.

A face looked back. A human face, inches from his face. He was so startled he backed away and fell off the narrow ledge.

Landing clumsily, he looked up at the glass. The thin, pale face remained, grinning with high amusement. Joe stood staring, his whiskers trembling, his paws growing slick with sweat. It was the man, the same man. Beckwhite's killer.

He could smell freshly cut wood; and beneath the window shone a raw scar where a screwdriver, or a hand drill, perhaps, had pierced through.

Realizing the man would soon have the window open, he spun around and made for the kitchen. Leaping at the closed door he yowled and scratched until Barney, the golden, woke bellowing, then Rube began to boom. Their combined warning shook the house.

But there was no sound from the bedroom; likely Clyde hadn't even stopped snoring.

And then, at a break in the dogs' barking he heard a car start. He raced to the front window, and leaped up.

A dark car was pulling away without lights. It spun a U, slowed going past the house, then moved out fast, and was gone. Far down the block it switched on its headlights, flashing suddenly onto the tree trunks and bushes as it swept past.

The street lay quiet. The killer was gone.

Up and down the street, the neighbors' windows were all dark. The oak trees stood black against the slowly fading sky. Joe sat down in the middle of the worn rug, where the threads were showing, and licked at an imagined flea.

But it wasn't a flea, it was an involuntary twitch generated by fear. He was nervous as a mouse in a tin pail.

This was just too much. This attempted break-in was the last dog hair in the milk bowl. His digression from normal cat had left him a bundle of raw feelings anyway. Now, this confrontation was more than he wanted to deal with. More than he knew how to deal with.

Needing human company, he jumped down from the sill and returned to the bedroom, to Clyde.

And, of course, Clyde had slept through it all. He was still snoring, relentless and loud as a chain saw. Joe wanted to crawl under the covers and snuggle in safety next to Clyde's warm, bare shoulder.

But he couldn't cower in bed, protected by his master. That was the behavior of a scared kitten, not of a grown tomcat. Tomcats in their prime were not supposed to be afraid. He hunched down on the Sarouk rug beside the bed.

This rug was the real thing. Small, hand-knotted,

and expensive. It had been a gift from one of Clyde's more serious lady friends. It offered a most satisfying texture in which to knead his claws.

He kneaded with a vengeance, working off fear and frustration, digging and pulling, trying to think what to do.

Beckwhite's killer had taken the trouble to find him, either by driving the village streets until he spotted him, or maybe checking with the local vet to see who owned a gray cat. Why? Did he think a cat was going to testify in court? His interest paralyzed Joe.

He watched an anemic dawn creep across the closed blinds, turning them the color of a brown paper bag; then suddenly the clouds parted, the sun's first rays burned against the shades, their golden blaze spilling underneath, picking out Clyde's jeans and sweatshirt, turning the worn Sarouk rug as red as the bloody entrails of a jackrabbit. The mockingbird tried again to sing, all grating sharps and flats.

He had told Clyde nothing of his problems. His housemate had no hint of his amazing verbal skills. So Clyde could know nothing about his witnessing the murder. And Clyde, preoccupied with that same murder, distressed by the loss of his business associate, had hardly noticed Joe's confusion.

When Joe had first realized he could understand human speech, he convinced himself that all cats had the same talent. That the ability was simply unused, that cats ignored human speech as too distracting.

But he knew better.

And then, when he realized that he could speak as well, he was so unnerved that he hid in a hole in the basement wall, cowering within the cold, hard concrete concavity, shivering with alarm.

He did not come out in answer to Clyde's shouts from upstairs, not even to Clyde's supper call. When Clyde found him and tried to haul him out, he lacerated Clyde's hand.

Afterward, he was ashamed. But he hadn't come out. He remained in the hole in the concrete for a full night and day. Clyde, always considerate, had left food and water for him on the floor below, but Joe didn't touch it.

When at last he did come out, and slaked his thirst before going upstairs, he had convinced himself this was a good thing, that he would be the envy of all other cats. A veritable feline king. He had talked himself from a gripping horror into a huge ego trip.

He immediately sought out his feline housemates, and tried his new talent, speaking to the other cats in human words, keeping his voice soft and his phrases tender.

"Come on, Snow Ball, come give us a little snuggle. Come on, Fluffy, come share the kibble, come have a little snack with a friend."

They were not amused. Their eyes grew huge and horrified; their hair stood up, their tails stiffened with alarm, and they hissed and ran from him.

When he tried talking to his current lady love, the results were disastrous. She slashed his nose, ran up a tree onto a roof, and had not come near him since.

She had taken up with an unspeakably scruffy orange tomcat.

No cat he encountered could comprehend the simplest sentence of human speech. Other cats knew only, *Come, Kitty,* and *Supper's On.* They understood human tone—anger, love, human voice inflection, human body language. Nothing more. When he spoke to them they responded either by running away or attacking. After several fights, he gave up.

And, of course, he didn't try talking to the household dogs. What would a dog know? Then last Sunday he discovered that not only could he understand and speak the language, he could read.

All his life he had been staring at cat food cans, pacing around them waiting for someone to fetch a can opener. But on Sunday morning, as he clawed open the cupboard and knocked a can out and watched it fall to the floor, then jumped down and stood over it yowling for Clyde, the words on the label began to make sense.

St. Martin's fresh ocean salmon, he had read. *This product prepared especially for the household cat.*

Clyde was incredibly slow on Sunday mornings, lingering over the papers unwashed and unshaven. Joe had waited impatiently, mewling and reading the recipe for his breakfast, *Fish parts, wheat flour, sardine oil,* and so on. Nothing wrong with fish innards.

Realizing that he was reading, alarmed and shaken with delayed shock, he had raised his voice louder in a panic of demand until Clyde came to open the can.

In a frenzy of hunger, needing sustenance for spirit and soul, he had devoured the contents in three huge gulps. Afterward, as Clyde held him, not knowing what was wrong but stroking him, trying to calm him, he had belched fish redolently into Clyde's face but he had not, definitely not, spoken any human word of apology.

Then soon after breakfast he had begun to experiment, stalking the newspaper and reading at random. The political columns didn't interest him much, but the advice column was a laugh. Who, except humans, could drum up such complicated intrigue over the simple question of sex? He had glanced over the obituaries and society page without interest, then abandoned the newspaper as unworthy of a feline.

On the couch he found the program from a play, and this was mildy interesting. Then in the bedroom he discovered a collection of steamy personal letters tucked into a half-open drawer. This was more like it. He clawed them out and spent a good hour poring over the contents, grinning.

Now in the brightening bedroom he watched intently the swiftly flitting shadows of birds in the tree outside, leaping from branch to branch. So simple to think only like a cat hungering after bird flesh, and not one beset with human complications.

But that simple distraction no longer worked. The birds seemed distant and frivolous. As frivolous as he had once thought words printed on paper were, silly and pointless. When he was a kitten, seeing Clyde stare at a printed page, he had felt ignored

and indignant. Clyde's inattention had made him
crazy.

Though, of course, that view had changed quickly
enough when he realized there was something magic
in those little marks, something that would cause
Clyde to talk endlessly to him, supplying long, comforting intervals of soothing human voice.

He paced the bedroom thinking about the hours
he had spent curled up beside Clyde as Clyde read
aloud from a great variety of novels.

How amusing that neither he nor Clyde had
understood that, as Joe listened and stared down at
those little black marks, he was learning things no
cat ought to know.

But though he considered his sudden ability to
read a feline breakthrough, even that was not the
most alarming aspect of this new and puzzling life.
The distressing part was, he not only had talents
like a human, he was thinking like a human.

For several mornings he had awakened planning
his day, wondering if it would rain and spoil the
bird hunting but drive the moles out into the open,
wondering whether the blackbirds were still feeding
on the pyracanthas behind the house. Blackbirds got
rolling drunk on the fermented pyracantha berries
and were ridiculously easy marks. He would wake
wondering if the cute little Abyssinian female down
the street was in season yet and if her owners would
let her out.

Cats didn't plan their day. Cats just went out and
did cat things. But not him. He woke in the big
double bed beside Clyde carefully laying out his

day like some grotty old banker marking his office calendar.

Take, for instance, this very moment. Any normal cat would be caught up in the immediacy of winging bird shadows, clawing open the door to get out. Instead he was crouched on the bed analyzing his thoughts in a manner abhorrent to feline nature.

He wondered what would happen if he spoke to Clyde about this. What would Clyde do? Could Clyde help? Maybe try to explain the phenomenon?

Sure. In a pig's eye.

If Clyde knew he was sharing his house with a talking cat, he'd likely throw him out, tell him that if he could talk, it was time he quit freeloading. Tell him to go join a circus.

He had lived with Clyde for four years, since Clyde found and rescued him when he was lying fevered and sick in a rain gutter.

Clyde Damen was an auto mechanic, he had the most prestigious shop in Molena Point, working exclusively on foreign cars, ministering to Molena Point's BMWs and Rollses. He rented his huge shop space from the Beckwhite Foreign Car Agency. He liked rodeos, football, baseball, and liked to watch newsclips of long-ago boxing events; Joe Louis was his hero—he collected Louis memorabilia. On the nights he didn't date or play poker, he read: thrillers, mysteries, and some remarkable books that didn't seem to fit his character. He told his girlfriends that he could write a really clever mystery if only he had the time. Joe's opinion was that Clyde didn't have the discipline for writing, that he had the curiosity and the wild twist of mind, but not the patience. Being a writer seemed to Joe a matter of taking things apart and putting them back together in new ways. Any cat could understand that kind of thinking. Clyde had the talent; but he just couldn't sit still long enough to be a writer. If you wanted mouse for supper, you had to stick to the mouse hole.

Joe smiled. He might criticize Clyde, but the truth was that he owed his life to Clyde. Born behind a row of overflowing garbage cans, the first of a litter of five kittens, Joe had learned early to fight for what he needed, to challenge what he feared, and to outsmart what he couldn't defeat. He had tolerated the alley just long enough to learn to get along in the world, then had inflicted himself forcefully on the first family he encountered, following two ragged children up three flights of tenement stairs. There he subdued the children's bulldog, then charmed the animal until it became his champion. It was in this home that his tail had been broken when the drunken master, coming in from a poker game, stepped on him in the middle of the night.

He left that place fast, and for good. Within days, his tail was infected. It throbbed, and it wept pus and smelled bad. He took refuge in a sewer opening, but he was soon too sick to find food. Burning with fever, he was unable even to creep out to search for water. He was soon dangerously dehydrated, confused, and disoriented. Late one afternoon, he awakened from fevered sleep to feel hands on him. He was too weak even to fight. Hot and aching, he felt himself lifted and carried. He heard the man muttering, but only much later did he identify Clyde's muttering as baby talk.

Clyde had put him in a car. He'd never been in a car but he recognized the stink of gasoline and tires and was horrified. That was his first car ride and his first visit to a veterinarian. Lying on a hard metal table he had felt himself prodded and manipulated, then felt the sharp prick of a needle in his rump. Soon he dropped into blackness as deep as a sewer excavation.

He knew nothing more until he woke in a cardboard box, lying on something soft that smelled of the same man. The room was pleasantly warm, and smelled of dogs and of frying steak, too, like the restaurant near his home alley. He was so weak he couldn't even get out of the box. It was when he turned to lick the pain in his tail that he discovered he had no tail.

His tail was gone. He had only a one inch stump.

But he could still *feel* the whole tail. And it hurt like hell. He had stared unbelieving at the raw stump, at his maimed, ugly backside.

For weeks the loss of his tail had badly screwed up his balance, to say nothing of his dignity. But, though the vet had amputated his tail, Clyde had not permitted the man to castrate him, for which Joe was eternally grateful.

When he had gained back some strength and gotten used to going without his tail he began to feel at home with Clyde. He liked Clyde's bachelor ways, and he sure didn't miss his last, drunken master or the noisy children. He soon set Clyde's household to rights, compelling the other three cats to obedience and subduing, then making friends with, the dogs. He had thought that this home with Clyde was his final, permanent home.

Now, that was not to be. Everything in him said: Get out. Run. He knew the man would return. And after murdering a human, what was the life of a cat?

Very likely, if he remained in this house, the killer would harm not only him. If Clyde tried to protect him, he would attack Clyde. What difference was one more blow to the head, after the first?

He washed his paws and face, smoothed his whiskers. But as he headed for the living room and his cat door, he was trembling. Though he felt goaded into flight, he felt trapped, too, by the world which lay beyond his own familiar realm, by the huge and complicated human world.

Crouched before the plastic rectangle of his cat door, he tried to prepare his thoughts for departure. For loneliness, and perhaps for death. Maybe this flight would be his last adventure, the culmination of a short and eventful feline career.

As the sun crept up above the neighbors' houses, and the translucent plastic of his door turned pale, Joe pushed it open and peered out.

Seeing no one in the yard, he thrust his head and shoulders out into the cool morning and looked along the house to the right, studying the bushes, then looked to his left. When he felt that all was clear he came out, did another quick scan of the street, and took off running.

3

The brindle cat was a thief, a charming, insouciant little thief quicker and more agile than any human criminal. She enjoyed, far more than any human burglar, her carefully selected prizes—she liked to fondle and sniff the silk nighties she stole from neighboring houses, and she would rub her face for hours against a purloined cashmere sweater. Among the modest, tree-sheltered cottages of the hillside Molena Point neighborhood where Dulcie lived, she was known affectionately as the cat burglar.

She was a petite little cat, a dark brown tabby, her swirled stripes streaked with a soft peach shade, the two colors forming patterns as rich as silk batik. Her pale muzzle and ears were tinted a delicate tone of peach, her soft belly and paws were peach. She was a charmer, an artfully colored little beauty.

She was a young cat, too, and sprightly as a young girl. She had an impish, upturned pink smile, when her white whiskers would stand up like signal flags. Her green eyes were so intelligent that tourists wandering the village would often stop to stare down at her, puzzled and arrested by the questioning tilt of her head and her bright green, inquiring glance.

Dulcie belonged, as much as a cat can belong, to Wilma Getz, a spinster of middle years, a retired probation officer currently employed by the Molena Point Library. Wilma was constantly amused by Dulcie's thieving. Sometimes, rising early to enjoy a cup of coffee before an early walk along the sea cliffs or up the beach, Wilma would, standing at the window sipping her coffee, see Dulcie coming across the yard dragging behind her a pink bra or a dark lace nightie, the little cat pulling the garment resolutely through the dew-soaked flowers. Then in a moment Dulcie would come pushing in through her cat door, dragging her prize.

Inside the kitchen she would drop the pretty garment, nose at it, and smile up at Wilma with delight.

Who could scold her?

Usually Wilma was able to return the stolen items to their rightful owners, digging out a necktie or a bikini top from beneath her couch or from under the claw-footed bathtub. She was far more lenient with Dulcie than she had ever been with her former clients. Never had she overlooked a parolee's or probationer's theft.

Wilma Getz was a tall, lean woman, with long gray hair she kept bound back in a ponytail. Her collection of silver and gold hair clips were of great interest to Dulcie; her jewelry box was an area for the cat's eager and delighted exploration. Wilma had been with Federal Probation until her retirement at fifty-five, an enforced retirement because of hazardous duty. She had been known among her caseload as hard-assed, an officer to pay attention to, or to be avoided.

Now that she had moved into a gentler life, with no more parolees to worry over, she could indulge her softer instincts. Could be far more lenient with her one remaining custodial charge, her loving and thieving small cat.

How could anyone scold the innocent young cat for her miscreant ways? Dulcie was so excited, so thrilled with each new acquisition, hugging and rolling on the soft, bright prize. What harm did she do? She was never malicious—her thefts grew from her pure delight in the stolen object.

Wilma kept a big wooden box on her covered back porch, and there she placed Dulcie's trophies so the neighbors could retrieve them at their convenience. Wilma Getz's back porch was known as the repository for all small, cat-sized lost items.

Because a steep hill rose behind the house, Wilma's cottage had been designed so both the back and front porches faced the street. Access to the back door was easy, the neighbors had only to come across the south end of the front yard on the winding stone path, step up under the wide roof into the deep back porch, and there root among Dulcie's treasures to retrieve their stolen garments.

Dulcie loved that box. She liked to curl up in the box among the silk and satin and the occasional finds of velvet. There, lounging on her silken contraband, she could watch the neighborhood, could see everything that went on, dogfights, ball games, the comings and goings of all the humans in her world. She did not seem to mind when a neighbor came searching for her own possessions. Dulcie would purr happily while the neighbor rummaged among the purloined sweaters and nighties, and she usually got a nice pet and a scratch behind the ears before the lady went away carrying her treasure. And before long she would find a new item to replace the one retrieved.

Dulcie knew how to get into every house in the neighborhood. She could claw open a window left ajar, could claw open a back screen door. She could leap to snatch and turn a doorknob. Molena Point was quiet, well policed; the village houses were often left unlocked in the daytime.

Dulcie, once she had gained entry to her chosen mark, would head for the bedrooms. There she would lift a pretty sweater she found lying on a chair, a slipper, a baby bootie, whatever took her fancy. With delicate paws she would remove a silk stocking from a bathroom rod where it had been hung to dry, carry it gently home, and hide it beneath the bed, where she could lie with her face on the silken gauze, purring. One young neighbor wore black satin mules that were a favorite. Dulcie took them and Wilma gave them back, but in over two dozen exchanges Dulcie never left a tooth mark on the satin. Once she entered the Jameson house at dinnertime and snatched a linen napkin from the lap of five-year-old Julie; she raced out brandishing the napkin like a flag, with the five Jamison children screaming after her in delighted pursuit.

When she stole the pink cashmere sweater that ten-year-old Nancy Coleman had bought by laboriously saving her allowance, Dulcie didn't know how Nancy suffered. Dulcie was a cat—she had no comprehension of the world of finance.

Though deep within, she sensed that taking the possessions of another was wrong. Every young cat learns quickly about territory by being slapped by larger, stronger cats. Territory should be respected. And Dulcie knew that *things* were territory, too.

But she stole anyway, with the same impish delight with which she would have taken another cat's bed. Stealing was a game. She stole smiling, her pink mouth curved up, her green eyes shining, her brindle tail twitching with pleasure. She once brought home a designer teddy trimmed with gold lamé and sequins. But Wilma took that away from her and returned it, wet around the edges from Dulcie's licking. Another time she stole a crocheted doll dressed in red leggings. She still had the doll, hidden in a dark corner of the service porch. She liked to hold it between her paws, purring.

She was quick to leap through an open car window, too, taking whatever treasure caught her fancy, audiotapes, baby rattles, driving gloves. She was so secretive about her thefts that the neighbors seldom saw her take an item. Though an early riser like Wilma might spot Dulcie dragging something pretty across the dewy lawns, perhaps a silver spoon left on a backyard picnic table, once a small porcelain cup with bright flowers glazed on it; she got the cup all the way home unbroken and hid it under the footed bathtub. From this crevice Wilma resurrected, as well, the watch for which she had mourned for a year—and had railed at Dulcie with untypical anger.

But she could not stay mad at Dulcie. The little cat was entirely joyful in her acquisitions, so happy with them, and sprightly as a little elf. When scolded she would cock her head and smile. Wilma sometimes brought home little treats for her, a lavender sachet, a lace handkerchief, items she knew would delight Dulcie. When Dulcie saw there was a gift she would sit up on her haunches, waving her paws and reaching, her pink mouth curved up with pleasure, her green eyes so intelligent that Wilma wondered sometimes if Dulcie could be different from other cats. The rapport between them was deep, loving, and comfortable. Wilma thought, *If I were rich, I would give her diamonds. Dulcie would wear diamonds.* In the six-block area where Dulcie had established her territory, the little cat was laughed at and loved, and certainly no one would harm her.

Beyond the hill where Wilma's house snuggled among oak trees and other cottages, stretched an undeveloped expanse of steep bluff that looked down on the sea. To humans this was an open, wind-tossed field. To the village cats it was a jungle, the heavy grass waving high above. Within the tall grass roamed a wealth of field mice, moles, grasshoppers, and small snakes. There Dulcie hunted. Or sometimes she simply sat concealed in the blowing grass, looking out toward the sea and listening to the pounding of the great mysterious water. The rhythmic thunder of the surf seemed to Dulcie like a loud purr or a steady heartbeat, and she would imagine herself a kitten again, snuggling secure in the thunder of her mother's purr. To Dulcie the sea was rich and wise. It was there, sitting concealed in the rye grass late one afternoon, absorbing the sun's warmth, that Dulcie realized she was watched.

A man watched her. She could smell his scent on the wind, sour and strangely nervous, a predatory smell like that of a hunting animal. She rose slowly to look above the grass, flinching with apprehension.

He stood above her up the cliff, where the sidewalk cut along: a lean, pale, shaggy man staring down directly at her, his muddy eyes chill and predatory. He watched her as intently as a crazed dog will stare. And in his eyes she glimpsed a brazen familiarity. She sensed that he could see deep inside her, could see her secret self. She crouched, immobile and rigid.

Dulcie had never been hurt—she had grown up with Wilma from the time she left her mother. No one had ever been mean to her, but she knew about cruelty and hurt. She had seen neighborhood animals hurt. She had once seen some boys beat a dog. She had seen out-of-town children kill a cat. Now she smelled the same scent, smelled the man's lust, and she knew beyond doubt that he would harm her.

Half of her wanted to run, half wanted to remain still, clinging to the earth as a baby animal will cling to avoid detection.

When she was hunched down deep in the grass, she couldn't see him. And she could hear no movement above the wind and the pounding sea, could hear no hush of footsteps approaching.

Yet she sensed that he drew closer. Her heart seemed to knock against the bones of her chest, drowning whatever sound might come to her.

When she could stand her apprehension no longer, again she rose up on her hind legs to look.

He was almost on her. He lunged, reaching. She spun away and ran. He came pounding behind her, she could hear the grass swishing against his pant legs, could feel the earth shake beneath his running feet. She sped along the edge of the cliff, terrified that if he couldn't grab her, he would kick her over the edge. Running, panting, she glanced down that fifty-foot drop, and her terror fuzzed her vision so not even the ground was clear. Her sucking breath burned in deep shudders.

4

Joe trotted fast up the wooded hills, up between scattered houses through their lush, overgrown gardens, and up across fields of tall, wild grass. He didn't think he was followed. But he didn't pause, either, until he stood high on a ridge among a forest of Scotch broom and rhododendron bushes. There, slipping in among their thin, tangled trunks, he thought he was safe, that no one would find him.

From the shadowed bushes he could see far down the slopes. Down beyond the tops of massed trees and roofs gleamed the sea, its bright surf spewing up white foam.

He had come up on a long green shoulder of land which rose abruptly above a broad valley to the south of the village. He was headed toward the wild upper slopes, toward scattered, newer houses and a few rich estates. Up beyond those, beyond the last houses, rose the wild, dry mountains of the California coastal range. High above him, the deep blue sky was alive with wheeling clouds; their shadows raced past him across the dropping hills.

He moved on again, upward, streaking up a grassy hill through running shadows.

But fear ran with him, too. He had to pause repeatedly and look behind him down the hills, afraid that he was followed, searching for that thin, hunched figure.

And, already he missed his home.

Gripped by an uncharacteristic attack of homesickness, he crawled deep into a stand of tall grass and lay with chin on paws, caught in a heavy depression quite unlike himself.

He was bitterly lonely, he felt totally cut off from the world.

He had been forced to abandon his warm, comfortable home, his neighborhood territory, his entourage of warm and adoring females. Forced to abandon everything that gave his life meaning. He'd forsaken Clyde's comforting care, Clyde's rude, good-natured teasing, as well as the small circle of household animal friends, the dull-minded but faithful dogs, the other cats, who, terrified of his new talents, had been remarkably obedient to his wishes. The cats now backed away groveling when he took the best morsels from their food plates. They were perfectly willing to sleep in a little cluster, allowing him to stretch out full length on their bed for an occasional nap. He was more than top cat, he was exotic and inexplicable. It seemed a shame to abandon all that fun.

But he was no longer one of the group, either.

He was separated from his own species by an abysmal void. He was not only torn away from his home and his family, he was, as well, a veritable alien in the cat world.

He couldn't even share his misery with another like himself.

There was no other.

Congealed by gloom, he crouched among the grasses, still and rigid, his white paws pressing into the earth, his eyes closed, a small bundle of cold despair.

Not since he was a half-grown kitten had he found himself totally alone.

And as a kitten he hadn't given a damn. What had he cared for loneliness? He'd stormed out of the cheap apartment where his tail got broken and to hell with human companionship. To hell with any companionship. He'd wanted only to be out of there. He had stalked away to challenge the world, unwise and untried, but brave as hell.

Now he was a totally different cat. That courageous youngster was gone. He was no longer a brash and nervy challenger; he was frightened and shaky, half-crazed with uncertainty. Totally unlike himself.

But soon a small voice nudged him. A deep disgust at his own cowardice.

He sat up, his ears back, his eyes blazing. *What kind of idiocy is this? What's the matter with me? Beaten? Uncertain? What the hell!*

The only thing wrong with him, he was hungry. He needed food. He hadn't eaten a thing since that mouse last night. His cowardly terrors would vanish the minute he took in some fuel.

A good feed, plus the satisfying ritual of the hunt, that was all he needed.

He reared up, scanning the tangled hillside.

All up and down the hill there was movement in the grass, where little invisible creatures were hopping and pecking and fluttering. Fixing on a half-seen sparrow that dabbled unaware, he crouched and began a measured stalk, his lips drawn back, his teeth chattering softly, his ears flat to his head.

Within seconds he had caught the unwary bird and torn it apart. He consumed it with satisfying greed, spitting out beak and feathers and feet. By the time he had caught and eaten a blackbird, he began to feel better.

When at last he was filled with the rich, lean meat, he was himself again, the blood leaping through his veins hot and predatory. His cathood restored, he drank from a puddle, looked around at the bright world, pricked his ears, lifted his short stub tail, and trotted on up the hill.

At the crest stood a broad oak hanging over a weathered cottage. Joe studied the branches for another cat. When he saw none, he took possession. Leaping up the trunk, he dug in, and climbed on up to the first good limb. It was level, broad, and perfect.

He seldom napped on the open ground. It wasn't smart, in the wild hills, to nap where a dog could surprise him.

In the yard below, a broken tricycle lay rusting among a patch of ragged daisies. He could hear a child laughing inside the house.

From high in the oak he could see down the

receding hills of Molena Point, the grid of half-hidden streets, the courthouse tower, the shops half-obscured by the oaks and eucalyptus. Beyond the village, the sea rolled against the cliffs in a long line of breakers, crashing up and sucking back in a rhythm as measured as his own purr.

Up here, he was king of all he could see. He could live up here, looking down like a god on the village, gorging royally on birds and squirrels, on endless meals of chipmunks and fat mice. If he was destined to life alone, this was the place to live it. Here he could be as strange and different as he pleased, and there was no one to care. He was his own cat, in a rich and fecund Eden.

The main street of the village, running inland from the beach, was clearly visible, with its green, parklike divider and broad, golden-leafed eucalyptus trees marching up its center. To the left of the median, the cottage rooftops snuggled close together. He couldn't quite see his own roof, but he could see his street. All was homey and familiar.

Perched up here, he was poised between two worlds. The village and hills were a cat's paradise. But behind him to the east, where the mountains of the coastal range lifted against the sky, that was not his world. Those forbidding, rocky cliffs presented a realm far more bloody and cruel. He really didn't care to become an hors d'oeuvre for the coyotes and pumas that hunted those mountains.

At least he had the sense to know the difference. Yawning, he stretched out along the branch, full and content. And he slept.

* * *

The crackling of dry grass woke him. He thought immediately of a prowling puma. Something heavy moved below him at the base of the oak tree, and he shook away the sleep, staring down between the leaves.

Dogs. Only dogs. Ugly and predatory, but just dogs. The five stupid canines circled his tree, ranging through the tall grass, nosing and huffing as they picked out his scent. Two were huge, brown shaggy beasts. One was a misshapen boxer, one a weasel-faced black bitch. The smallest, a spotted terrier, looked up and saw him and began to yap.

The boxer stared up, and let out a bellow that bent Joe's eardrums.

In an instant all five were barking and clawing at the trunk. He eyed them with disgust and considered dropping down on their tender noses.

But not even he was fool enough to take on five dogs at once, four of them the size of small ponies. He thought for a minute, glancing toward the cottage.

He saw no movement behind the cottage windows, no sign that anyone was looking out. When he was certain that he was unobscrved he slipped out along the branch nearly to its tip. The dogs went crazy, roaring and leaping.

At the end of the branch, Joe paused. The dogs bellowed and jumped. He opened his mouth in a broad cat smile.

"Go home!" he yelled. "Get the hell out of here!"

The effect was memorable. The dogs jerked to attention, staring around for the human source.

"Get out! Get the hell home!"

They stared up at him. They backed away crouching, their ears and tails low, their lips pulled back in rictuses of fear.

"Go on, you mangy mother-licking retards! Get yourselves home!"

They turned as one and ran careening in a tight, frightened pack. Skidding and sliding, they disappeared down the hill.

He smiled, licked his whiskers, and stretched. Whatever the source of his unusual talent, it had its upside. Yawning, he washed a paw, then curled up on the branch again and went back to sleep.

When he woke at dawn, the world was drowned beneath a sea of fog. The hills were gone, all of Molena Point had vanished. He gazed out over the white surface at scattered treetops rising up in dark, shaggy islands.

He was hungry, and he was stiff. The tree branch, though safely off the ground, was not as kind to the body as a well-appointed double bed with its clean sheets and soft blankets and the warmth of Clyde next to him.

Clyde would be waking now. He'd feel around on the bed for him. He'd call him. When he realized there was no tomcat nearby, that he'd been gone all night, he'd stagger out to the front porch to call him, shouting across the sleeping neighborhood—as he had undoubtedly done several times during the night.

When no cat appeared, he would swear, pull on some clothes and, unwashed and unshaven, gulp a cup of coffee and go to look for him.

Joe had awakened twice during the night, the first time because he nearly fell off the branch. He had started to roll over, and only the jolt of the tree limb under his shoulder had jerked him fully alert. The second time he woke, the fog was rolling in, hiding the stars. He could not remember his dream, except that eyes watched him.

He shook his whiskers, washed his face and ears, and inspected his claws. He licked his stub tail then backed down the tree to hunt. It was while hunting that he figured out, in a flash of inspiration, how to keep Clyde from worrying.

Stalking the fog-shrouded bushes, he scented a wharf rat and tracked it. But though he was careful, he came on the rat unexpectedly. It was waiting for him, rearing up, its little red eyes blazing. He got only a glimpse as it leaped into his face.

They met tooth to tooth in midair. Before he could claw it away it had bit and raked him. It tore his cheeks and nose, just missed his eyes. He ripped it off, biting and clawing and at last got it by the throat and killed it.

He ate the rat, then licked the blood from his wounds, grimacing at the bitter, ratty aftertaste. Rats were never sweet like bird or mouse. He drooled cleansing cat spit onto his paws and cleaned blood from his face, and cleaned the wounds the little beast had inflicted. And he thought longingly of canned tuna, of the luxury of eating prepared tuna from his own plate, on his own chair at the kitchen table beside Clyde.

Boy, have I gotten soft.

But face it, he missed the little luxuries of a cozy home.

Maybe he missed home so sharply because he'd been driven out against his will. If he'd simply left for a ramble of a few days, the matter would be totally different. Choice was the thing. The freedom to choose when he wanted to leave and to choose when he wanted to return home.

Suddenly he wanted his own chair by the window, the chair which he had rendered over his four-year tenure into a frayed and comfortable nest overlaid with escaped feather stuffing and with a fine patina of his own gray-and-white fur. He wanted the comforting smells of home, too, the smell of Clyde's morning coffee, of frying hamburger, the ever-present smell of dog and of onions and beer. He even missed the smell of Clyde's feet.

Right now, this minute, Clyde was out searching for him, muttering, 'Damn cat. Damned useless cat,' walking the neighborhood yelling his name, asking the neighbors.

When he didn't show up, Clyde would phone the pound or go over there. That was what he did when the white kitten was lost, and that was where Clyde found her, locked in a cage; Clyde brought her home mumbling baby talk, and fed her on steak for a week.

He felt bad that Clyde was worrying. He valued Clyde. He and Clyde were buddies. He was the only cat of the household that Clyde allowed in bed, the only cat who ate his dinner on a chair next to Clyde's chair. He and Clyde were pals. He knew how to get a laugh out of Clyde, and Clyde knew how to get a smile out of him. He didn't like to worry Clyde—Clyde fretted over his animals. They were all the family he had.

He wanted to go home. And he couldn't. He was alone with this and he would remain alone.

Until—when?

Until he got rid of his pursuer.

A rising wind parted his fur and nipped at his ears, and began to tear apart the fog, lifting and shredding it. One thing he could do—he could set Clyde's mind at ease. He just needed to figure how to let Clyde know he was all right. Reassure Clyde, let him know he was safe and not to worry.

Well, so he'd phone Clyde.

The idea exploded like a light bulb blazing on, as in the funny papers. A light bulb over the cat's head. He'd call Clyde. Tell Clyde he was doing okay.

Fired with inspiration, he moved away from the gnawed rat bones and stood up on his hind legs, stretching up tall to study the scattered hillside houses. All he needed was a phone. Slip into a near-by house through an open window or claw a hole in the screen, find a phone, and call Clyde. Why not?

Sure, and what if he was discovered, and the window slammed shut by an irate homeowner, trapping him inside? Trapped among strangers.

He looked down the hills, through the last thin wisps of fog, at the toy-sized village far below, at its shops crowded along the main street. Shops with phones, shops sparsely staffed this early in the morning, shops with wide, frequently opened doors through which to escape.

It might seem like walking back into the jaws of the dilemma. But he'd feel easier in those public places with plenty of foot traffic going in and out, plenty of hurrying feet which he could race past, to freedom.

He set off at a gallop down the hills. Streaking down through tangled yards and across narrow little streets, he swarmed away from several roaming dogs, and narrowly avoided colliding with a delivery truck. He soon hit Ocean Avenue.

The sidewalk was wet from the fog, the air sharp with the scent of eucalyptus from the long double row of big trees marching down the grassy, parklike center between the eastbound and westbound lanes. Trotting down the sidewalk, he wondered if he could handle a phone, if he could manage to punch in the numbers.

The doors of the shops were just being unlocked, the shopkeepers looking out through the glass, jangling their keys. A young man in jeans ran past as if he were late for work. And Joe hurried along himself, watching warily for the killer. And watching for Clyde. Just his luck if Clyde decided to have breakfast in the village and saw him.

He could never explain why he couldn't come home. Clyde would snatch him up and carry him home forcefully, or try to. And while the thought of home was more than appealing, he was convinced that home was now a death trap.

In front of the little market, the greengrocer was arranging apples in a bin, the scent of apples sharp and sweet, mixed with the smell of celery. The scent from the fish market was sweeter. But he didn't go near; he headed straight for the pharmacy.

Approaching the doorway, he dodged a departing woman, who pounded along in a pair of red high heels. He could see the druggist way at the back, behind a glass partition, filling orders. The shop was empty, no customers now. And he knew from listening to Clyde that old Sid worked alone, that the old druggist had solitary ways.

He could see the telephone up on the soda fountain, near the door. He trotted on in and slipped behind the counter, stood concealed within the dim space. Glancing down its length, he could still see white-haired Sid back there, intent on his little bottles. He was filling them from big bottles, sending a stream of pills rattling through a funnel. The old man was short, thick-limbed, and Joe knew that his hearing wasn't keen. There were village jokes about Sid's fanciful translations of what he thought he had heard. The doctors of Molena Point never ordered a prescription by phone; always their messages were written, committed illegibly to little white slips of paper.

On a shelf beneath the counter, wedged between a box of bills and a pair of Sid's white oxfords, he found the telephone book. He clawed it out, broke its fall with his shoulder to dull the sound, and let it slide to the floor.

It took him a long time to fork the pages open to the D's, then to find the right page for Damen. He felt stupid because he didn't know the alphabet. But at last he found Clyde Damen, and, with the number firmly in mind, he jumped up onto the counter.

Gripping the cord in his teeth, he lifted the receiver off the hook and laid it silently on the pale marble surface. The phone's push buttons were a cinch, once he figured out how to squinch his paw real small. Crouching with his ear to the receiver he listened to the phone ring.

It rang a long time. This was Saturday, Clyde always slept late on Saturdays. Or maybe he was in the shower. Or maybe he had a sleepover date. When a woman spent the night, Clyde made Joe endure the indignity of sleeping in the kitchen.

On the twelfth ring, when Clyde answered, panic hit him. What was he going to say? He couldn't do this, this was insane. He didn't know what to say.

"Hello?" Clyde shouted again. "Who is this? Speak up!"

Joe couldn't speak, couldn't even croak, his throat was dry as feathers.

"Who is this?" Clyde yelled. "Say something or hang up, it's too early for games!"

"It's me," Joe said, swallowing. "It's Joe Grey."

He was certain that the minute he spoke, the pharmacist would hear him, but at the back of the store the old man didn't look up. He could hear Clyde breathing.

"It's me. It's Joe—it's really me. I thought I'd better tell you why I left, yesterday morning."

No response.

"I thought you'd want to know I'm all right. I thought maybe you'd be worried, looking for me."

Clyde shouted so loud that Joe hissed and backed up, his ear ringing. "What kind of sick joke is this! Who the hell is this? What the hell have you done to my cat!"

"I *am* your cat," Joe said softly. "It's me. It's Joe. The tomcat who put three permanent scars on Rube's nose and tore a patch of hair out of Barney's muzzle that grew in black instead of brown. It's me, Bedtime Buddy. Rakish Ruckster," he said, repeating Clyde's stupid pet names. "Favorite Feline."

Through the receiver, he heard Clyde swallow. This was a blast. "Listen," Joe said, "do you remember yesterday morning when I was wiggling around under the covers, then I got down and I was sort of mumbling to myself? Do you remember what you said?"

Clyde's breathing was clearly audible.

"You said, 'For Christ sake, Joe, stop it! It's too damned early to be horny!' Then you went back to sleep, and the window shades were getting light."

There was a very long silence. Joe watched the pharmacist. The old man had heard nothing. His gray hair caught the light as he bent over his work wiping up the counters. At the other end of the phone, Clyde seemed to revive himself. "How—how did you know . . . Who the hell is this! How did you . . . ?" Then, after another very long silence Clyde said, "What—what is your favorite breakfast?"

"Cream and Wheaties with chopped liver," Joe said, grinning. "No one," he said, "no one could know that but me, buddy."

"Who was—who was my date two weeks ago Friday?"

"Eleanor Hoffman," Joe said. "Blond. Blue eyes. Little gold lace dress short enough to show her underpants, and a giggle like a steam train. I don't need to tell you, Clyde, I don't like that woman. She woke me up at three in the morning singing her insipid songs. It sickens me to watch you in the shower washing her back."

The silence threatened to stretch into Monday. Then Clyde said, "If it's really you, where the hell are you? I'll come get you."

Joe licked a bit of rat fur off his lip.

"Well, where? And why the hell did you leave! How come you can use the phone and you never told me? *How come you can talk? How come you never told me you can talk?*" There was another silence, then, "Christ. This can't be happening. And isn't this house good enough for you? Just because you can talk, you think you're some kind of celebrity?"

"I can't come home. Someone is following me."

"What? What do you mean, following you? Who would be following you? What's going on? Where the hell are you?"

"I—Trust me," Joe said. "When I get this sorted out, I'll be home."

He licked his paw. "I want to come home," he said in an uncharacteristic moment of sentimentality. "I guess I miss you."

A movement caught his eye. The pharmacist had started up the aisle beside the candy counter. "Gotta go," Joe hissed. "I'm okay—be in touch." He leaped from the counter leaving the receiver off the hook and fled through the open door. Old Sid saw him and shouted. "Scat! Scat! Get out of here!"

He sped across the street directly into the path of a pickup full of firewood. He managed to dodge it, feeling the heat of its wheels. He gained the curb, panting. Leaping across the sidewalk to the grass, he turned east, moving fast up the tree-shaded median.

Within minutes of talking with Clyde he was out of the village again, headed up into the hills, still tense with fear but grinning with amusement.

5

Dulcie raced along the top of the cliff nearly swept off by the wind, wind pushed and shoved at her pressing her toward the fifty-foot drop. Far below her the sea heaved and crashed; and the man running behind her drew closer, forcing her toward the edge. In another instant he'd reach her and kick her over, down the jagged rocks. She was blinded by flashes of sunlight and by the swift shadows of racing clouds. Along the cliff's ragged edge, she couldn't be sure where the land fell away beneath her flying paws. The man was nearly on her; suddenly he kicked out at her.

She dodged, twisting away, leaped over his foot, and dived into a tangle of heavy weeds.

Crouching within the frail shelter, she stared out between the brittle stems.

But as he lunged at her she spun away again, fleeing away through the grass forest, heading for the street. Heading back toward houses and sidewalks where there might be people, where she might find shelter. Leaping across the sidewalk into the street, she didn't see the car. Brakes screamed, a horn blared. She dodged into the path of a truck coming in the other direction, and felt its heat as she skinned to the far curb.

The man had careened away to dodge the truck. She flashed across a lawn toward a line of bushes beside a tall yellow house. Diving into the shrubbery, she felt her heart pounding like the heart of a terrified mouse when she caught it, fast, too fast.

And again the man was on her as she plunged into the bushes; he snatched her by the tail, jerking her painfully off her feet. She flipped over yowling and dug in her claws, raking and biting his arm.

He dropped her, swearing. She twisted away tasting his blood. Racing along the perimeter of the house beside a row of basement windows, she stopped and doubled back.

One window was ajar a few inches. She flung herself at the glass. The hinged pane gave. She leaped into black, empty space.

She dropped half a story, landing hard on a concrete floor. The fall jarred her legs and shoulders and bruised her tender paws. Crouching, she turned to stare up at the window.

He knelt above her, peering in. She fled into the cellar's black depths, into the farthest corner, and hunched down, panting as he reached through.

His pale hand groped. He pushed the window wide, and swung his legs through. As he prepared to jump down, she ran blindly; and rammed her shoulder into a sharp corner.

Pain took her breath and made her eyes water. Dizzied, sucking in air, she saw that the corner belonged to a stairway. As he landed on the concrete behind her, she leaped away up the steps.

High above her, the basement door stood ajar. She careened up and through as he hit the stairs, her frantic paws slipping on the bare wood.

She stood in a hall. To her left, sunlight blazed through the glass of the front door. But the entry was too light, too open. As she swung away toward the next flight, the basement door slammed behind her. He had blocked her retreat. Running, she hit the next flight of stairs.

The pale tweed carpet was thick, and gave good traction. Her claws dug in, sent her flying up two flights, then three. The stairs slowed him. She could hear his labored breathing.

At the top of the third flight a door barred her way. The stairs ended. A high little window in the door was filled with blue sky.

She leaped at the knob, grabbed it in scrabbling paws, but it wouldn't turn. She swung and kicked, but thought it was locked. He was on the flight below her. She jumped higher, against the glass, and could see a flat roof stretching away.

He exploded up the last flight and lunged for her. She flew at his face raking and biting, kicking, clawing. He grabbed her trying to pull her loose. She bit him harder and jumped free, fled past him as he clutched at his face.

She hit the steps halfway down, flew down the treads hardly touching them. Down and down, with the man crashing down behind her, the thud of his weight as he hit each step seemed to shake the whole house. At the bottom she swerved past the closed basement door into the bright entry.

A parlor opened on her left, and she glimpsed wicker funiture, splashes of green. To her right, tall double doors were closed. She could hear kitchen sounds beyond, could hear pots and dishes rattling.

The front door had no knob, but a latch one would press, and a long brass handle below it. She was crouched to leap for the latch when she heard children laughing, pounding up onto the porch. The door flung open.

She careened out between their legs amidst surprised shouting, felt little hands on her back, then she was through, diving into sunlight, then into shadow beneath a parked car.

She heard him shout at the children, heard him running, watched his feet approach the car. She ran again, doubling back between the yellow house and a white one, and scrambled over a fence.

She dropped from the fence into a tiny yard full of scattered toys abandoned among the rough grass. Behind her, he came over the top of the fence sucking for breath. She glimpsed his eyes, pale brown and glistening with rage. His face was red with his efforts, and bleeding. She streaked away over a second fence and through another yard, taking heart from the wounds she had inflicted. On she ran through uncounted fenced yards, not looking back. She heard him for a while running, and then silence.

She slipped under a porch and looked out.

She thought he was gone. She heard nothing. The yard before her remained empty, its deep flower beds and neat lawn tranquil and blessedly vacant beneath the warm sun. She was nearly done for, panting and heaving. Cats were made for short spurts, for the quick chase. Long endurance was a dog's style. When she was sure she had lost him, when he did not appear from around the side of the green frame house, she trotted quickly away toward home. Longing for home, for the safety of home, her ears turning back to catch any small sound behind her.

Soon she was on her own street—she could see her own house, its pale gray stone rising so welcoming and solid from Wilma's lush English garden. Once she was inside those walls, nothing could reach her. She fled the last block mewling, passed the front porch, and flew up the back steps and in through her cat door.

Wilma was in the kitchen. She stared down at Dulcie, and grabbed her up, holding her close, stroking her. Dulcie trembled so hard she couldn't even purr, could only shiver against the thin old woman.

Frowning, Wilma stepped to the window and stood looking out at the street.

"There's nothing out there," she said, staring down at Dulcie, puzzled. "Was it a dog? Did a dog chase you? I've never seen you so afraid." She set Dulcie on the kitchen table and examined her, feeling along her body and her legs looking for wounds. When Wilma's probing fingers touched bruises, Dulcie winced. She examined each hurt more carefully, gently feeling for broken bones.

"I don't think anything's broken." She said at last. She looked at the dried blood on Dulcie's paws, then pressed so Dulcie's claws were bared. She grinned at the amount of blood. "Looks like you got in some licks of your own, my dear."

She carried Dulcie into the living room, to the couch, and wrapped the blue afghan around her, cuddling and stroking her.

Under Wilma's tender ministrations, Dulcie began to relax. This was so nice, so safe and comforting. She was home. Wilma loved her. She nosed into Wilma's warm hand, and a purr started deep inside her, the same deep, reverberating thunder she'd experienced as a kitten when she was totally protected and loved.

Purring, curling down wrapped in the soft wool, she didn't stir as Wilma left her and returned to the kitchen. She heard Wilma open the refrigerator, and soon she could smell milk warming.

Wilma brought the bowl to the couch and held it as Dulcie lapped. She'd been terribly thirsty. She gulped the milk down, nearly choking. The afghan was so warm around her, the milk so heartening.

When the bowl was empty she closed her eyes. Her paws and tail felt heavy but her body seemed weightless, as if she were floating.

She slept.

For some time after the little cat slept, Wilma sat beside her puzzling over what might have happened. She had found no open wound, no bite mark, no

real indication of a cat fight. She didn't understand
what those strange, hurt places were on Dulcie's
body, little areas tender as bruises.

Whatever had happened, Dulcie had certainly
bloodied something. She hoped she did a good job
on the creature.

The little cat was no slouch in a fight. Dulcie
could hold her own with most dogs. And she wasn't
always on the defensive, either. She had been known
to provoke other female cats unmercifully.

This little tabby was tough. Beneath that sweet
smile, Dulcie was tough as army boots. Before she
was a year old she had established in her six-block territory a realm of personal safety where no dog or cat
dared challenge her. No, whatever chased her today
must have been a stranger to the neighborhood.

When she was convinced that Dulcie was all
right, Wilma left the little cat sleeping and went to
get dressed. This was concert night. Tickets for the
short season of the village concert were sold out
months ahead, and tonight was a special appearance
of the San Francisco Symphony Orchestra present-
ing Schoenberg. She chose a full, flowered skirt and
a hand-knit top, the first dress-up clothes she'd had
on in weeks. As she opened her jewelry box and
selected a cloisonné clip to hold back her gray hair,
she half expected Dulcie to hear the small squeak of
the lid opening, and come trotting in. The little cat
loved to paw through her collection of barrettes;
bright jewelry fascinated her as much as did pretty,
soft clothes.

She heard no sound from the living room, and

when she looked in, Dulcie was deeply asleep, out like a light. As she left the house, she thought of locking the cat door, of keeping Dulcie inside. But the idea of a gas leak or of fire, with Dulcie shut inside, sickened her.

If whatever had chased her was still out there, Dulcie would know it. She'd stay in. Or she would go only onto the back porch, where she could see the street but slip quickly away, back into the house.

She drew the draperies in the living room and dining room, and in the kichen she pulled the curtains, wondering why she was taking such care. Whatever had been after Dulcie wasn't going to be looking in the windows. Half the time she left the curtains open at night, as did her neighbors. She'd gotten spoiled, living in Molena Point. Spoiled and soft. In the other towns where she had lived, she had always covered the windows at night.

She opened a can of salmon, Dulcie's favorite, and emptied it into Dulcie's clean blue bowl. But she didn't leave it in the kitchen; she hated to smell up the house with fish. She set it out on the porch, just outside Dulcie's cat door, where she would find it when she woke.

She went on out the back door, locking it behind her, and along a little stone patch to the attached carport.

Backing out of the drive she looked carefully around the yard and along the street for strange animals. Heading down the hill toward the village, she watched the sidewalks, but she saw nothing unusual, no strange dogs. Only one man out walking, a thin, stooped figure walking away from her. She didn't recognize him, at least not from the back, but the village was full of tourists.

Dulcie woke three hours after Wilma left. She knew at once that the house was empty by the quality of total silence, the air congealed into absolute stillness, a dead response to her seeking senses which occurred only in an empty house.

She prowled the rooms for a while, looking up warily at the windows. Wilma had drawn the draperies before she left. Usually she forgot. Twice Dulcie leaped up under the draperies, crouching on the sill to look out.

Each time she looked, beyond the cold glass the dark street was empty. And within the shadows of Wilma's front garden, no one was standing half-hidden. No one standing against the dark trunks of the oak trees; and the flower beds and stone walks were undisturbed by any intruder.

Of the houses across the street, three were dark, and five had lights on. At the Ramirez house the porch light burned as if the young couple was expecting company. The Ramirez's were one of her favorite families. Nancy Ramirez wore the prettiest silk nighties; and usually she left the back door unlocked.

She jumped down from beneath the draperies and warily approached her cat door.

The carport light shone in through the plastic. She sniffed the cold evening air that seeped in around the free-swinging door. She couldn't smell the man, but she did smell salmon. Wilma had left her a nice bowl of salmon. Ravenous, she pushed out onto the porch.

She studied the yard and street briefly, then dived for a bite of the nice red fish.

A rank smell stopped her. She stared at the dark, rich salmon, and backed away. It smelled bitter.

The salmon smelled of death. Of poison. Her nice supper had been poisoned. She stood staring around the dark yard, sick with anger.

She knew about poison. The neighbor's collie died last summer after eating a dead rat. Dulcie had approached the body of the unmoving dog where it lay sprawled across the lawn of the neighbor's house. The time was dawn, the sky was hardly light. She was the first one to find the dog; it would be another hour before the family rose and discovered him there.

She had stood beside the rigid beast, shocked. She had never seen a big animal dead, only birds and mice. He was so still, his body so unlike the dog she had known. Empty. Horrifyingly still and empty.

She had liked that collie; he was always kind, he never chased her. Shivering, she had crept closer to the unmoving beast. She didn't have to stretch forward to touch him, to know that he was dead, to know the hard, stiff, dry condition of what remained.

His spirit was gone. His tan-and-white body was nothing but a heap of fur. The sweet spirit of the collie had fled.

She had crept closer at last, and smelled the collie's face, sniffed at his mouth.

He smelled bitter. A foreign, metallic bitterness.

Exactly like her salmon. She could taste the smell.

The thin, hunched man had done this. Had poisoned her supper.

A growl rumbled deep in her throat. She hissed at her supper bowl, then put her shoulder against it. Pushing, she shoved it across the porch and over into the pansies.

Jumping down, she dug a hole and pushed the bowl in—her dear blue bowl, that she loved.

She buried the bowl and the salmon deep, pawing flowers and earth over the mess, stamping the dirt down with hard, angry slaps.

Finished, she scented along the steps and soon found the man's sour smell. She followed it. Ears back, tail jerking with rage, she tracked him across the garden through a low bed of leafy ajuga and along the sidewalk. Above her across the dark sky, clouds had rolled in to hide the moon. Following his trail, thinking about the poison, and thinking about his flying feet hazing her along the cliff, she flinched at every shadow.

Trotting up sidewalks and through gardens, she studied all the black concavities in the neighbors' dark yards, but she saw no unfamiliar shape, only the black silhouettes of bushes and trees. But his scent was there, on the sidewalk. She followed it for two blocks before she lost it among car smells and the reek of dog pee. And even after the trail had vanished she pushed on.

She didn't know what she meant to do if she found him. Sure, go for his throat. But her rage wouldn't let her rest. Her poisoned salmon was the last straw.

Near to midnight, when at last her anger had cooled, when she calmed, and admitted the odds, when only her fear remained, she crept into the bushes to hide and rest. *This is really not smart, to be out here alone,* she thought. Not when he was probably lurking somewhere near, or would soon return to make sure she was dead.

She rested fitfully, startling at every tiny breeze. And when, half an hour later, she heard Wilma's car pass on the street she rose eagerly and started home.

She was three blocks away when she heard Wilma pull into the drive, then heard the back door open and close. Then in a moment the front door opened, and Wilma was calling her. She let out a little responsive mewl, burst out of the bushes, and ran eagerly.

But as she passed a line of parked cars, she smelled him. She veered away, but he appeared from beside a carport, slipping out into the night. She ran.

Wilma called her again as she bolted away through the bushes—away from the man, but away from Wilma, too. Away from home.

She could not go home. Why had she thought she could go home?

He knew where she lived. Neither she nor Wilma would be safe. As he gave chase again, she streaked straight uphill between close-set cottages, flashing up across the narrow village streets wondering if she must run forever. Heading higher, for the wild hills, she prayed she could lose him for good on the tangled, overgrown slopes.

6

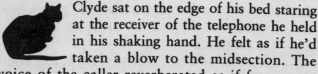
Clyde sat on the edge of his bed staring at the receiver of the telephone he held in his shaking hand. He felt as if he'd taken a blow to the midsection. The voice of the caller reverberated as if from some unseen dimension, replaying back to him an impossible message.

It's me. It's Joe Grey . . . I thought you'd be worried. . . . I am your cat. Bedtime Buddy. Favorite Feline. . . . Cream and Wheaties with chopped liver . . . I don't like that woman. It sickens me to watch you in the shower washing her back . . .

Some joke. Some twisted, sick joke.

Who had that been? Whose voice was that? Which one of his idiot friends? Who had the talent to pull off that kind of phone call? To make it sound so much like Joe Cat, and to tell him that personal stuff. Who *knew* that personal stuff? Who did he know who could pull that off, and not break up laughing?

He dropped the phone on the bed and stood up, looking around the dim bedroom. The rush of adrenaline generated by the phone call was making his stomach flip.

The drawn shades were awash with sunlight, bright rays creeping in around the edges.

He turned, stared at the phone. Maybe the phone hadn't rung at all. Maybe he'd dreamed that it was ringing. Probably he'd dreamed the whole damned conversation.

That was it. He'd dreamed that the phone rang, and he snatched it up in his sleep. He'd dreamed he was talking to Joe. That had to be the explanation. The only logical explanation. It couldn't have been one of his friends; no one else knew the things the caller had told him.

And no one—no one in the world could know exactly what he had shouted at Joe yesterday morning when Joe was pacing and muttering. *For Christ sake, Joe, stop it! It's too damned early to be horny!* No one in the world could mimic the exact, irritated sound of his own voice at that precise moment, his own angry, half-asleep growl.

It had been a dream, a figment conjured out of his own warped mind.

For a minute there he'd really bought it. He could still hear the caller's voice, so familiar, rasping and coolly amused, its harsh tone exactly like Joe Cat's insulting yowl.

He got up, staring at the phone, then picked up the receiver and dropped it back in its cradle.

But the next instant he snatched it up again and threw it on the rumpled bed. He didn't want it to ring. He wasn't answering any more phone calls. The receiver buzzed for a moment, then a taped female voice told him to hang up and dial again.

"I didn't dial!" he shouted at the taped voice. "And you can go to hell!"

He had to have some coffee. And he'd better get in the shower, get dressed for work.

It took him several minutes to realize that this was Saturday and his day off, that he'd still be asleep if Joe hadn't called.

If Joe hadn't . . .

He'd better get hold of himself.

Cats did not make phone calls.

Cats did not speak human words.

Cats communicated with body language. Cats said things with angry glares, with tail lashings and butt wiggles. They let you know how they felt by squinching their ears down or poking you with a paw. By hissing at you, or flipping their tail and stalking away. That was cat talk. Cats did not speak the English language.

He stood scratching his stubbled chin, knowing in his gut that the phone call hadn't been a dream. Knowing that the ringing of the phone *had* waked him. Remembering the sunlight slashing beneath the shade into his eyes as he rolled over and grabbed the phone. Hearing that rasping voice.

The morning sun beat relentlessly against the window shades, thrusting its bright fingers more powerfully underneath like some nosy neighbor. His face itched; he hated it when his face itched. Staring at the demanding sunlight, imagining the bright day beyond the blinds, he got an unwanted mental picture of Joe stretched out in the sunshine somewhere, maybe beside someone's pool, talking over the poolside phone.

He flipped up a window shade, causing the stiff fabric to spin dangerously on its roller. He stood at the window, staring out at the street praying he would see Joe come strolling down the sidewalk.

And knowing he wouldn't.

Where the hell was the cat?

He needed coffee. He needed to talk to someone. He needed to see if the rest of the animals were different this morning.

What was he going to find in the kitchen? A tangle of chattering dogs and cats complaining about the quality of their breakfast? Bitching because he was late getting up?

He shuffled down the hall in his shorts; as he opened the kitchen door, a barrage of leaping canines hit him. The two warm, whining dogs pummeled and pushed. The cats yowled and wound around his bare ankles, tickling with their twining, furry greeting.

Neither the cats nor the dogs spoke a word. All remained satisfyingly mute. He petted Rube gratefully. The black Lab smiled up at him, then bent to lick his toes. Barney pushed against them both, growling as he competed for attention.

He scratched the dogs until they calmed down, then picked up all three cats, cuddling them in a huge hug, letting them rub their faces against his bristly cheeks.

When the cats began staring down from his arms at the counters, looking for some sign of breakfast, he put them down again on the floor. Stepping over the furry tangle, he filled the coffeepot with water and got the can of coffee from the cupboard. But he was still so upset by the phone call he spilled half the coffee grounds, then lost count of how many scoops. He ended up dumping it all back in the can and starting over.

That call was the perfect end to a rotten week. First the break-in at the shop, when his automotive tools were stolen along with a collection of shop gauges that would be hard to replace. The senseless burglary enraged and puzzled him. The thief could just as easily have entered the main showroom instead of the shop, could have broken the lock on the big showroom overhead doors and driven off with several million dollars' worth of new, and vintage, foreign cars.

Why, with that fortune sitting in the showroom, had he chosen to burgle the shop?

Then three mornings later, Max Harper had shown up at the agency just before opening time, and that was when the real nightmare began.

The police chief had pulled his patrol car into the covered drive between the showroom and the shop. Harper's thin, lined face had been more than ordinarily glum.

He'd known Max Harper since they were in high school; they had done some ranch work together, summers, and had rodeoed together, riding the bulls. Harper had joined the police force after four years at San Jose State. He'd married while still in college; his wife, Millie, had been in the criminal justice program at San Jose, too, and had gone into law enforcement. She died two years ago, of a brain hemorrhage. The

pain of her death was still raw for Harper. You could
see it hidden behind his natural wariness.

Harper didn't get out of the squad car, but sat
behind the wheel frowning at him. "Beckwhite
won't be in this morning."

"So? How come you're relaying the message?"
But he'd felt a chill begin. "What happened?"

Harper reached into his uniform pocket for a
pack of cigarettes, and shook one out, and gave him
a level look. "Beckwhite's dead. He was killed last
night." Harper watched him carefully, at the same
time seeing every movement within the shop where
three mechanics were laying out tools preparing for
their morning's work.

His first thought, a trite reaction, was that
Beckwhite couldn't be dead, that he'd seen Beckwhite
only yesterday. No, any minute now Beckwhite
would come strolling into the shop from the showroom, carrying a paper cup of coffee from the
machine, his close-cropped military haircut catching
a gleam from the overhead lights, his grin self-satisfied
even at this early hour. No, Samuel Beckwhite wasn't
dead.

"George Jolly found his body this morning, in the
alley behind the deli. He'd been hit on the head, his
skull cracked." Harper struck a match and cupped
his hand around the flame, though there was no
wind. He blew smoke out through the opposite window. "No sign of anything that Beckwhite could
have hit his head against. And it was too hard a
blow for that. The coroner's looking at it. He's been
dead since eight or nine last night."

It had taken him a while to respond. "Has—has someone told his wife? Told Sheril?"

Harper nodded. "I went on up there." He got a funny look on his face, but said nothing more.

The shock of Beckwhite's death had left the agency staff confused, had thrown the conduct of day-to-day business into chaos. The murder had been all over the papers, local and San Francisco.

And the murder, for various reasons, had left him feeling uneasy. That unease was heightened considerably when, yesterday morning as he was looking for Joe Cat, he discovered that someone had tried to break into the house through the living room window.

When he saw the splintered wood, he had barged outdoors in his shorts and found a larger hole on that side, ragged and broken as if gouged by a tire iron or by a large screwdriver.

He had hurried back inside, staring around the living room. Nothing was gone—TV and VCR were there, CD player, all the electronic equipment. And then, because Joe Cat wasn't nearby yowling for his breakfast, he grew concerned for all the animals. He headed for the kitchen; but when he flung open the kitchen door, the dogs were rarin' to go, charging past him straight for the living room. Leaping at the window, roaring and snarling, they had put on an amazing surge of adrenaline for two fat old farts.

The window was so freshly splintered that it still smelled like new lumber. He had found no other damage to the outside of the house, and no sign that anyone had gotten inside. When he checked the study, nothing was amiss. The one item that concerned him was still on the desk, the small note-book lay in plain sight beside his checkbook. He had stuffed it under some papers, intending to hide it later.

The attempted burglary, just after Beckwhite's death, had disturbed him enough to make him load the .38 snub nose he kept for traveling, and slip it into his night table. He could not help equating the burglary in some way with Beckwhite's murder.

He'd known Samuel Beckwhite for six years; they were business associates though he did not work for Beckwhite. He rented the big repair shop portion of the agency in exchange for maintenance and repair on the agency's foreign cars, and he serviced the vehicles belonging to the agency's regular customers. A friend from his high school days, Jimmie Osborne, had brought him and Beckwhite together originally, suggesting the business arrangement. Jimmie was agency manager; he had worked for Beckwhite since a year after Jimmie and Kate were married.

He never could figure out why Kate had married Jimmie. Golden-haired Kate Anderson had been some catch for sour, humorless Jimmie Osborne.

Standing in the kitchen waiting for the coffee water to suck up into the machine, he finally real-ized he hadn't turned on the coffeemaker. He flipped the switch, the red light came on, and the machine gasped a pneumatic wheeze. He yawned and adjusted his binding shorts. He hadn't slept well. Every little noise had brought him up listening for the scrape of claws or the slap of the cat door.

And of course the early phone call jerking him from sleep, and that rasping voice, hadn't helped.

I am your cat . . . *It's me, Joe Grey.*

Forget it. Get your mind off it.

He removed the glass carafe and poured a cup of coffee, but the machine hadn't quite finished. In insolent defiance at his meddling it dribbled coffee down onto the heating unit. The animals kept pushing at him, wanting breakfast.

He wondered who would eventually take over at the shop, or if Beckwhite's would be sold.

Jimmie Osborne was next in command, though Sheril Beckwhite, of course, was the new owner. Since Beckwhite's death, the office was chaotic. No one seemed able to carry on efficiently. There were endless glitches in the paperwork, unnecessary rewriting of sales contracts. And the relationship between Sheril and Jimmie didn't add to agency morale. Who could have confidence in Jimmie's managerial functions when they were conducted mostly in bed?

Everyone knew about the affair. He'd wondered whether Beckwhite had known. He felt sure that Kate didn't know. Kate wouldn't dream that Jimmie would cheat on her.

He wouldn't have remained friends with Jimmie, except for Kate. He and Jimmie had had little in common, even in high school. But he enjoyed Kate, saw things in Kate that Jimmie didn't see or didn't care to see. She was wry and funny, and he liked her comfortable empathy for animals. She really loved his two old dogs and the cats, and she shared with him a kind of warped, animal-centered humor that bored Jimmie. He and Kate always had a good time together, while Jimmie yawned.

He would never overstep the bonds of friendship with the Osbornes, he had never touched Kate. But she was beautiful and fun to be with, and without Jimmie their relationship might have evolved into a good deal more.

It surprised him sometimes that Jimmie put up with their evenings together, with their potluck barbecues and casual spaghetti dinners; and with the animals, particularly the cats. Jimmie said he was allergic to animals, but he never sneezed. The animals avoided him, though, all but Joe Cat.

Joe always went straight to Osborne the minute they arrived, rubbing against his pant legs, methodically covering Jimmie's freshly cleaned slacks with gray and white hairs. And Joe liked to sit on the couch beside Jimmie. He would remain close as Jimmie fidgeted. But before Jimmie got up the nerve to shove him off he would leap on the coffee table, deliberately spilling Jimmie's drink.

Cats loved to do that stuff—they found high amusement in tormenting those who disliked or feared them. And Kate watched Joe's pranks with a little secret laugh. Though she would never deliberately hurt Jimmie.

Given Kate's beauty and charm and her obvious enjoyment of life, he thought it incredible that Jimmie would pursue this affair with Sheril Beckwhite. Some men couldn't deal comfortably with the blessings of a beautiful wife; they had to find a cheap stand-in, someone flawed to make them look better by comparison.

He had known about the affair for months. He'd been surprised when Jimmie called him four times this week, looking for Kate, saying she hadn't been home. He was surprised that Jimmie would care enough to call anyone. He hoped Kate had finally left Jimmie, and not just gone down to Santa Barbara as she sometimes did, to get away.

Kate deserved better than Jimmie Osborne, her blond good looks and blithe spirit and her bright outlook were wasted on Jimmie. He thought sometimes that Kate's perceptive, almost fey qualities frightened Jimmie.

He refilled his coffee cup, letting his thoughts return to the subject he'd been avoiding, playing over again in his mind this morning's phone call. *I can't come home. Someone is following me . . . Trust me. When I get this sorted out, I'll be home. I am* your *cat . . . I guess I miss you.*

The dogs pushed against his bare legs, demanding breakfast. He pummeled them absently, letting them chew on his hand, then opened the cupboard and lifted out assorted cans. If Joe Cat were here he'd be up on the counter clawing open the cupboard himself, yowling and raking cans onto the floor, his bomb raid narrowly missing his companions, though they knew to stand out of the way.

The shaky feeling started again.

He needed to talk to someone.

Someone who wouldn't say he was nuts, who wouldn't laugh at him.

When the dogs had finished scarfing up Kennel Ration and began to slobber on him, smearing dog food down his legs, he pushed them outside into the backyard. The three cats looked up at the open door, but continued to eat.

The only person besides Kate who would listen to his crazy story about the phone call and not fall over laughing was Wilma.

He'd known Wilma Getz since he was eight, when her parents moved next door, up on Harley Street. She was in graduate school at USC, having returned to college after breaking off a bad marriage. She'd stayed with her folks during vacations while she interned in various law enforcement agencies. A tall, slim, stunning blond, she was his first love, her warm smile and her easy ways sending his eight-year-old libido into a wild juvenile spin.

Even then, when he was eight, Wilma had always had time to listen to him, always had time for a game of catch or to toss a few baskets in his driveway. Over the years, she had never lost her ability to listen and to ease him.

Wilma's passion for law enforcement had taken her from USC to State Parole, then to Federal Probation and Parole in San Francisco, and then to Denver. She had retired from the Denver office five years ago. Returning to Molena Point, she had gone to work in the understaffed village library, where her thorough, almost picky approach to a problem was put to good use as a reference assistant.

He had to talk with Wilma. There was no one else who, upon hearing his description of that phone call and the reasons why the caller couldn't have been any of his friends, wouldn't suggest an appointment with a local shrink.

He poured the last of the coffee and carried his cup into the bedroom. He phoned the library to see if Wilma was free for lunch, but she'd taken the day off. When he called the house, there was no answer. Annoyed, he decided to run by. Maybe she was only out walking. He hung up the phone, tossed his shorts in the laundry bag, and got in the shower.

7

At the foot of the Molena Point pier ran a boardwalk. The strip of muddy shore beneath it was never touched by sunlight. In that damp gloomy world under the pilings sour smelling puddles oozed, their surfaces scummed with green algae, their murky depths half-concealing empty, rusted beer cans and the sheen of broken wine bottles. A few boulders rose from the damp sand, and between these were strewn additional cans, fish bones, and sodden cigarette butts.

In the half dark between the puddles, the wet sand was crisscrossed with the pawprints of an occasional dog or with human prints, barefoot or with embossed rubber patterns. But the preponderance of prints were cat tracks.

Despite the damp, inhospitable environ, Molena Point's few stray cats considered the roofed shadows their own. They moved from the area only when forced out by children or dogs, or by desperate lovers with nowhere else to find privacy. Then, routed from their home, the cats crouched in the bushes at the edge of the beach, waiting patiently to return.

The area stank of dead fish and of cat. The cat colony was small, and these few thin beasts were the only strays in the village. They were fed weekly by one or two elderly villagers, but they made their meals primarily on fish offal carelessly thrown down from the dock above as village fishermen cleaned their catch.

None among the strays had the courage to cross the beach and make its way up the village streets to see what better fare, or perhaps a better life, might be available.

None of the lean, starving cats had any notion of the elegant repasts offered in the alley behind George Jolly's Deli. The mangy felines fought constantly over their meager fish scraps, and over the weekly, dry cat food. Sometimes a boy brought food, too, a skinny kid on a bike. He left not only cat kibble, but traps, placing several metal cages under the boardwalk, simple wire boxes with one-way doors leading in, but no way to get out. The cats were understandably wary of the arrangement.

But when all other food had been eaten, when they were desperate with hunger, one or two among them would chance the encounter, slinking in after the food. Caught there, the cat would eat his fill and then, unable to get out, would crouch in misery, though somewhat appeased by a full belly. Hours later the boy would return and take both cat and trap away with him.

The other cats didn't notice that one or several of their number had disappeared, nor would they have cared. They fought over breeding rights, fought for no reason, fought constantly for the best damp, cold niche between the boulders, in which to sleep or rest.

In a dark concavity between the bank and a wet piling hunched a cat so filthy she looked like old, used scrub rags. For uncounted days she had hidden beneath the boardwalk, sleeping on the mud, drinking sour rainwater, fighting the other cats for fish scraps and for a place to rest. She had no knowledge of how she had come there. Her pale, dirty coat and tail were matted with mud, and her fur was marked with strange rusty streaks, as if she had been crawling though the rusty drainage pipes which emerged at intervals along the shore, spilling gutter water into the sea. She didn't seem to care that she was dirty; she made no effort to wash herself. She avoided the other cats as best she could, and she stayed away from the gridded indentations in the sand, where the metal cages had stood, because the sand there smelled strange. Crouching alone, shivering, she huddled among the boulders hungry and confused.

This cat had no imprinted memories as would a normal cat, no recollection of an earlier life. No sense of where she had been before she came here. No reference of past, familiar smells or of remembered physical sensations. She did not remember ever being petted, had no memory of either stroking or of pain.

A cat's memory is built on shapes and sounds and scents, on the swift movement of prey, on images which speak directly to her senses. Cold stone beneath the paws, wet grass tickling the nose. A warm soft blanket beneath kneading claws. Hot concrete warming a supine body, hot tarry rooftops to roll on. Soft words, soft hands stroking, or cruel hands. Memory of a screaming voice, of rocks thrown at her; of the shouting and abuses of small boys. Memories of hunting: the swift dive of a bird on the wind, the warm taste of mouse.

This cat's memory held nothing. No lingering feline imprint of place or of experience. If she had a past, it was gone.

But she had retained one puzzling fragment: a recollection of sounds so alarming that when they assaulted her in half sleep she woke shivering and quaking. Sounds as unwanted as broken glass puncturing her paw, and she could not escape them. Within her confused memory, human voices spoke.

This was not the incomprehensible shouting of tourists on the walk above, or the softer voices of the village fishermen as they sat idly in the sun. These were words occurring inside her head, and they were spoken directly *to* her, as if she should understand.

The sensation was terrifying. But yet the voices touched something deep within her. When they spoke, some presence tried to stir. She was riven by fear, but she was nudged by something more, by a sharp anticipation.

But each time the voices spoke, her terror won the battle. Each time they spoke, whispering, beguiling her, she hissed and dropped her ears and tried to back away. Shaken by spasms of fear, she fled into the darkest shadows, where the ground rose to meet the wooden walk.

But she could not escape. The voices were relentless, as bold as the thin, wild cats which hazed her.

Thus without joy she remained beneath the damp walk, fighting her small, incomprehensible battles. Thus she might remain for the rest of her life unless the voices could reach her.

8

Joe lay atop the marble posterior of a naked lady, one of a trio of pale nymphs caught in eternal frolic in the center of a plashing fountain. The figure he had chosen leaned over to splash herself, providing him with a long, sun-warmed resting place quite protected from the bouncing spray. From her sleek, sun-warmed body, he had an unbroken view in all directions.

Surrounding the fountain was a half acre of private lawn sheltered on three sides by an eight-foot stone wall over which, at intervals, cup of gold vines were trained. On the fourth side of the smooth green stood a three-storied Tudor mansion. The handsome structure was steep-roofed, with four stone chimneys, and had heavy oak half-timbers set at the corners between the creamy walls. Joe could see inside through a set of deep French windows, a sitting room furnished with soft blue velvet settees arranged on a pale oriental rug. On the creamy walls hung bright California landscapes framed in gold.

The midmorning sun beat down on the smooth

marble, creating a little oasis of heat. Stretched out across the lady's smooth rump, he felt his short tail flick with lazy contentment. He yawned. The beauty of this arrangement was that, even if he napped, and even with the noise of the gently falling water, he would certainly be alerted to anyone coming over the wall.

If Beckwhite's killer came looking for him, a possibility extremely doubtful, the only other way in was up the drive at the far side of the house, or through the house itself. He had found, in this delightful setting, the perfect hideout.

And to cap it off, he'd never lived so well. He had landed in the lap of true luxury. He was so full of breakfast that he belched.

He had dined royally this morning courtesy of the elderly, round-faced housekeeper of the estate. She had served him leftover broiled salmon, a bowl of thick cream, and a selection of soggy canapés that included chopped goose liver and black caviar. Breakfast had been as fine a meal as he had ever been offered by George Jolly. Certainly it was far beyond the canned cat food that some people thought of as a suitable breakfast.

He had taken his repast on the side patio of the mansion, a wide stone expanse with a view of the eastern mountains. As he enjoyed his leisurely meal, the old woman pottered about nearby, watering her geraniums and singing little snatches of Irish ballads. She was a skinny little thing with a face like a ferret, but with a kindness for cats and with a sunny disposition.

Given the quality of the cuisine and the friendliness of the housekeeper and her husband, and the safety which the high stone wall afforded, the temptation to stay there was powerful. There was nothing to stop him from moving right in, establishing headquarters.

He could hear, at this moment, from around the side of the house, the voices of the housekeeper and her husband; the husband seemed to be the caretaker. They sounded relaxed and happy. Despite the elegant leftovers, they appeared to be the only humans in residence at the moment, and that suited him just fine.

Last night, when the housekeeper discovered him in the garden, she had seemed delighted with his company.

He had, growing tired of mice and birds, approached the back door, where he could smell a beef roast cooking. He trotted up the stone steps and stood looking in through the glass door, into a spacious kitchen and breakfast room. The breakfast room was done up in hand-painted tiles and flowered chintz, very bright and homey. His first mewl brought the old woman's glance from where she was setting the table.

She had opened the door wide. "It's a kitty. A stray kitty. Henry, come look." And she had invited him right on in.

The husband was a small man with a huge brown mustache and huge hands. To be stroked by those hands was like being petted by a catcher's mitt.

She did not offer Joe food until she had put supper on the table and she and Henry had sat down.

As she served the plates, she fixed a plate for him, too, much as Clyde would do at supper. Only this meal was out of Clyde's league. She put the plate on the floor beside the table.

That meal had been just as fine as this morning's breakfast, a slice of rare prime rib cut small and served warm and bloody, and mashed potatoes and gravy, all artfully arranged on a cracked, hand-painted porcelain plate. And for desert a dollop of rum custard.

A few days of this, and he'd be so fat he wouldn't be able to run from a one-legged turtle, let alone from Beckwhite's killer.

And yet despite the couple's eager goodwill, or perhaps because of excessive goodwill, their attentions had left him with a cloying discomfort. They had been so friendly that by the end of the evening, when he demanded to go out, he had felt pushed, felt leaned on. They had let him out with worried little flutterings about whether he would return, and the woman had put a cushion for him outside on a chair.

He ignored the cushion and slept on the marble lady. She held the day's heat until long after midnight.

But he dreamed that he was shut in a cage. And now as he lolled atop the fountain with little droplets of cool water bursting up around him, he began to feel watched. He felt a sudden powerful need to glance up toward the windows of the house. And he found himself flinching at every flick of a winging bird, startling at every blowing leaf, jumpy as a toad on hot pavement.

He stared down at the burbling fountain, blinking in the sun's bouncing reflections, trying to shake off his unease.

But he couldn't shake it, couldn't lose the feeling that those two well-meaning folks would soon get pushy, try to keep him inside by the hearth whether he wanted to stay or not. Try to turn him into a tame little lapcat.

He would like at least one more gourmet meal before he left the premises, but he wasn't going to chance it. It was time to go. Time to cut out. He leaped from the lady's marble rump straight across the pool, through the fountain's spray. Landing on the lip of the pool, he hit the grass running.

Streaking up the cup of gold vine and over the wall, he sailed down in one big jump, hit the woods running free, he was out of there. The leaves crackled and shook beneath his speeding paws, he charged at fallen logs and leaped them, drunk with freedom and speed.

But then, belting along through the woods, he began to think about Clyde. About how he missed Clyde.

He began to think about Clyde and the murder weapon.

Until that moment he had managed to ignore the possible connection of the killer's bright wrench to Clyde. But truth was, that weapon that killed Beckwhite had looked exactly like the new torque wrench Clyde had purchased only a month before.

The package had come to the house via UPS, had been waiting for Clyde when he got home from work. The wrench was handmade, by a craftsman in England. It might, Joe had thought, not be any more efficient than a plain, manufactured wrench, but to Clyde it was cast in gold.

And now, with the wrench stolen among an array of automotive tools, and undoubtedly with Clyde's fingerprints all over it, Joe could only wonder if the whole robbery had been for the express purpose of acquiring a suitably incriminating weapon; to wonder if Clyde was the patsy. If, when the missing weapon was found, Clyde might be taking his meals behind bars. Between the night of the murder, and the night when the killer tried to break into their house looking for a gray tomcat, the newspapers had been full of the murder. The weapon, 'Possibly a piece of metal, perhaps a length of pipe,' had not thus far been found.

None of it made any sense. But if he knew why the killer might want to frame Clyde, maybe he could piece together the scenario, maybe things would begin to add up.

One thing sure, if that *was* Clyde's wrench that killed Beckwhite, the cops mustn't find it.

He tried to remember if the killer had worn gloves to prevent smearing Clyde's prints, but he could not. He'd been too concered with saving his own hide.

He broke out of the woods on the crest of the hill, stood staring down at the village. Somehow, he was going to find that wrench.

Studying the roofs half-hidden among the trees, he tried to find his own dark-roofed, white Cape

Cod. To find a little glimpse of home. The time was midmorning, and it was Sunday. Clyde would be schlepping around the house unwashed and stubbly, probably still in his Jockey shorts, drinking coffee and reading the sports page. Barney and Rube and the three cats would be napping, either on their two-tiered bunk beds in the laundry or lounging in the sunny backyard.

He was scanning the village, trying to find home, when he glanced down and saw, among the low bushes, a caterpillar spinning its cocoon. Watching it, he was soon fascinated with how the wooly worm's body accordioned so the stiff hairs of its pelt shot left then right. Amazing how skillfully it spun its continuous thread from some wonderful machine in its innards. Excitement touched him, keen interest. He found himself observing the little worm in a disconcertingly unfeline manner.

He studied intently, details he had never before fixed on. Watching the little beast at work, he was caught in an unaccustomed fever of discovery.

Any normal cat would bat the furry worm and tease it, play with it, crush it, maybe taste it. Though caterpillars were incredibly bitter. But here he was, fascinated by the caterpillar's amazing skill. Its remarkable talent of spinning held him spellbound.

On and on it worked, spitting forth yards of silk, maybe miles of thin thread. The small animal humbled him.

And he realized, with one of those instant, earthshaking revelations, that this amazing little creature was far too cleverly conceived to have come into the world by accident.

This creature had evolved by some logical and amazing plan. Joe was observing one small portion of some vast and intricate design.

Right before his eyes he was watching a miracle. Nothing less than a boundless and immoderate creativity could account for the complex and efficient little beast working away beneath his nose.

He hunched closer, absorbing every detail.

And this productive little being was only one minute individual in a huge and astonishing array of creatures. He couldn't even conceive of how many beasts there were in the world, each with its own unique skills and talents. He trembled at the wisdom that had made caterpillars and cats, made dogs, birds, and lizards, made the whole gigantic world. It had taken a huge and astonishing intellect to conceive this endless array, an intelligence steeped in some vast mystery.

And I am part of it, he thought. *I may be strange and singular, but in some way I am part of the incredible puzzle.* Then he smiled, amused by his own unaccustomed intellectual excitement.

Your normal cat would be bored silly with such philosophical conjecture. Your normal cat would stalk off in disgust. A normal cat did not study small creatures with the wonder of discovery, but with an eye to the kill and to a full stomach. A normal cat majored in battle techniques and killing, not philosophy. A normal cat was concerned with the destruction of his prey, not with its meaning and origin.

But face it, he wasn't normal.

Life had been simpler when he hadn't had such involving thoughts; but it hadn't been as much fun. He liked his new ability to link ideas together—the possibilities held him drunk with power.

Only after some time did he shake himself and pay attention to his growling stomach. His inner discourse had left him famished; the mental exercise seemed as enervating as a five-mile run. Studying the hillside for fresh meat, he fixed on a nearby squirrel dabbling among the dead grass.

The squirrel watched him sideways, beady-eyed, shaking its tail in an irresistible flirt. The beast was fat beneath its fur; it obviously spent most of its time gobbling acorns from the abundant oak trees that shaded the hillside. The little beast's swift, jerking movements spoke to every fiber of Joe's cat spirit, drawing him into a crouching stalk.

But at his charge the little monster ran up a tree, leaped to the next tree, and was gone, leaving him empty-pawed and embarrassed.

He ought to know better than to chase squirrels. They always pulled that trick; flirt and scuttle around, luring a cat close, and then poof, up a tree and gone. And if a cat was fool enough to climb after it, the squirrel simply jumped to another tree. Or it fled high into the thin tiny branches that would break beneath a cat's weight, leaving the cat mewling with frustration.

Abandoning all thought of squirrel, he watched the grass for low-darting birds. When he spotted a towhee scratching in the leaves, he crept toward it, silent and quick.

But then, in pursuit of the towhee, he crossed the fresh trail of a rabbit. At once he forgot the trusting orange-and-black bird and set off after the succulent beast, tracking it uphill.

He didn't get rabbit at home; the neighborhood was too civilized. His hunting at home ran to birds, bad-tempered moles, and house mice.

The rabbit's fresh scent led him through the tall grass to the edge of a ravine and down, into a stand of massed oak trees. Among the dark trunks lay a heap of branches and leaves where a gigantic old oak had fallen, a grandfather among trees, its prone limbs as big around as the crooked legs of elephants in some exotic TV special.

Silently he slipped down following the trail. Very likely the little beast had dug his den beneath the dense tangles of dead leaves and massed branches.

Yes, the scent led right on in. He pressed into the dark jungle of dead twigs and dry leaves, squinching his eyes nearly shut to avoid getting jabbed.

Something stirred ahead, in the blackness. He froze.

Something was there besides rabbit, something intently watching him. Something far bolder than a rabbit. And whatever it was didn't mean to back off.

As he strained to see, two eyes appeared, catching the light, blazing like green fire.

Joe held his ground, scenting deeply, his nose and whiskers twitching as he tried to identify the creature, but he could smell only the rotting oak limbs and dead leaves.

The twigs and leaves crackled, and a small branch broke as the creature surged forward. Quickly he backed out where he had room to fight. He waited, crouched, his ears flat, his teeth bared in a cold grin.

The dry leaves rustled and shook and were thrust aside, and among the leaves appeared a small, triangular nose. Joe shivered, but now his trembling was not from fear. The green eyes slitted with amusement. He caught her scent now, delectable as sun-warmed clover.

She shouldered aside a branch and slipped out into the sunlight. Her eyes caressed him. Her little pink mouth curved up in a smile. She moved so near to him that he trembled.

She was delicately made, her dark tabby stripes rich as mink, swirled with pale tan and peach, her nose and ears tinted pale peach. She tilted her head, her look intelligent and challenging, filled with a keen curiosity.

Joe touched his nose to hers, breathing in her scent. Her warmth radiated through him like a hearthfire, and he matched his purr to hers. He longed to speak to her and knew that she would run or would swat him. He wanted to whisper love words to her, but dare not frighten her. He could only stare, purring inanely.

9

Sunlight turned the little cat's ears translucent, as pink and delicate as seashells. Her green eyes laughed. But her look challenged him, too. She stared at him intently, with a deep curiosity. Her gaze turned him weak, made him want to hunt for her, want to bring her exotic and succulent birds. He imagined capturing for her canaries and parakeets and white doves. He promised himself he would remain mute for the rest of his life if she would linger. He would never speak another human word, would do nothing to alarm her if only she would smile upon him.

Above them, clouds cut across the sun, sending shadows racing over them. In the suddenly diminished light the little cat's pupils grew huge and black, the bright green receding to thin jade rings. Then the shadows fled past, and sunlight ran in a river over her rich fur. Her eyes were bright emeralds again, wide and seductive. Her whiskers brushed his cheek, sending a charge through him as violent as the time he bit into the electrical wire.

She was a small cat, delicate and fine-boned. She

did not take her gaze from his, but she lifted one soft, peach-tinted paw. Her gesture imprisoned him. She cocked her head, her eyes questioning him so brightly that he couldn't breathe. Her pink mouth turned up in a smile of secret delight. He wanted to lick her delicate pink ears and nibble them.

But how nervous she was, her ears twitching forward and back at every stir of air, her body turning restlessly toward each innocuous rustle of small lizard or insect. And when a bird burst out of the bushes, she started and crouched ready to bolt away.

"No!" he cried. "Wait . . . "

He froze, horrified.

He couldn't look at her. He had done the unspeakable. He had given away his terrible affliction. In a second she would run from him. Or she would hiss and strike him, claw him. He turned away, ashamed. He'd blown it. He had irreparably, stupidly blown it.

But she didn't run. And she didn't move away. When he dared to look, her gaze was filled with amazement.

She didn't act like any other cat to whom he had spoken. Her eyes were wide and puzzled; but were bright with excitement, too. Her pink mouth was open. A soft panting trembled her throat. "What are you?" she said softly.

Joe's world reeled. He gaped. His heart seemed to stop beating.

"What are you?" she whispered. "What are we, that you can speak and I can understand?"

He was drowning with pure, insane joy. He pressed so close to her he could feel her heart beating against his heart. She sniffed his shoulder and mewled, her cry so soft it made his skin ripple. "What are we?" she said gently. "What are we, that is like no other?"

Still he couldn't reply. He could only stare at her.

She said, "You were there in the alley that night, you saw that man die. I saw you—you ran from him." Her green eyes narrowed. "He tried to kill you, he chased you. I wanted to help, but I was afraid. I thought about you—afterward. I prayed you were all right."

She had thought about him? His world tilted and spun.

"That man," she said, hissing softly, "that man did not kill for food. He did not kill as a cat kills. Nor did he kill to protect himself. He killed," she said, "not out of passion. He killed coldly. Not even a snake kills so coldly."

"You were there. You saw him."

"Yes, I saw him. And when he turned, he saw me. But he chased you—he couldn't chase us both." She laid her paw softly on his paw. "How can he know about us? But he must know, why else would he chase us, and follow us?"

"He's chased you? Followed you?"

"Yes. How does he know about us? How can he know that we could tell what we saw? Oh yes, he's followed me. He terrifies me. He almost caught me out on the cliff in the wind. He would have pushed me over. The smell of him makes me retch.

"But," she said, purring, "now we are not alone. Now, neither of us is alone.

"Now," she said, laughing, showing sharp white teeth, "now, maybe that man should beware."

Joe's purr shook him, reverberating uneven and wild. She made him feel as no other cat ever had. She made him feel not so much riven with lust, as turned inside out with joy. She smiled again and nuzzled him, her green eyes caressing him. And delicately she licked his whiskers. Life, all in an instant, had exploded from mere pleasure and excitement into a world of insane delight. Nothing that ever happened, from this instant forward, could mar this one delirious and perfect moment.

10

Kate Osborne had no memory of entering the dim, smelly alley. She had no idea where she was, she had never seen this place. There were no alleys like this in Molena Point, alleys garbage-strewn and as filthy as some Los Angeles slum.

A dirty brick building walled the alley on three sides. It was built in a U shape to nearly enclose the short, narrow strip of trash-strewn concrete in which she was trapped. At the far end, a solid wood fence blocked the only opening, its gate securely closed. She had no memory of pushing in through that heavy, latched gate though it seemed the only way in; unless she had climbed out into the alley through one of the closed, dirty windows.

None of the first floor windows looked as if it had been opened since the building was erected. The small, dirty, first floor panes were shielded by an assortment of venetian and louvered blinds as might belong to various cheap business offices. The dirty windows above—there were three stories—looked equally immovable. Behind their limp, graying curtains, she guessed would be small, threadbare apartments.

She stood in long shadow, as if the sun were low, but she couldn't tell whether the time was early morning or late afternoon. Around her bare, dirty feet were piled heaps of trash, overflowing from five lidless, dented garbage cans. Smelly food containers, dirty wadded papers, rotting vegetables. The stink was terrible.

She felt disheveled, dirty. Her mouth tasted sour, and she felt as if she had just waked from a terribly deep sleep and from a dream that she did not want to remember.

She was breathing raggedly, as if she had been running. Her poor hands were filthy, and she had two broken nails: filthy nails, black underneath.

A faint scent of ripe fish clung around her, but of course that was from the garbage; the smell made her gag.

She was not in the habit of being filthy. She must look like a tramp. She could work in the garden all day and not get dirty. She prided herself on her neatness, on her clear skin and her well-cut, simple clothes, on the sleek trim of her blond hair. Now when she touched her neat, pale bob it was tangled into a mess.

Her jeans were stained with what looked like rust, and quantities of damp sand clung to them. The long sleeves of her cream silk shirt were smeared with rust, too, and with black mud. She felt so hot and sticky. She never let herself get like this. Never. Even her toenails were black with grime; and her lips were dry and chapped.

Her last memory was of home. Of feeling clean

and well groomed, comfortable. She had been working in the kitchen, canning applesauce in her sunny, pale yellow kitchen, listening to old Dorsey tunes which had been reissued on CD—music recorded long before she was born, but music she loved. The cooking apples had smelled so good, laced with sugar and cinnamon. Their bubbling aroma, and the steam from the sterilizer had filled the kitchen like a warm, delicious fog. It was perhaps an old-fashioned thing to do, to put up applesauce. She and Jimmie had bought a bushel of winesaps up in Santa Cruz, coming back from a weekend in the city. She loved San Francisco. They always had a good time, but she'd been glad to be home again, tending to the simple chore of canning. It made her feel productive and useful, and the domestic endeavor always pleased Jimmie.

She could not remember sealing the lids or setting the jars to cool. She didn't remember anything after standing at the stove stirring the warm, cinnamon-scented apples.

She felt in her pocket for her house key, but found nothing, not even a tissue. She wouldn't have come out without her key even if she left the house unlocked—she had locked herself out too many times. She could not remember leaving the house. Why would she leave, when she was canning?

Somewhere, at the very back of her mind beyond what she could reach—or was willing to reach—a terrifying shadow waited to make itself known. She could feel the thrust of some chilling, unwanted knowledge. Something so shocking she didn't dare to know. She pushed the presence away, stood frightened and shivering and alone, staring at the dirty brick wall.

Something she dare not remember waited crouched and silent, at the very edge of conscious knowledge.

She studied the building more closely. In a way, it looked familiar. There was a dark brick building like this south of the village, near the old mission, a bit of ugliness left over from Molena Point's less affluent days. The space was rented, she thought, for small business offices. And probably there would be cheap apartments above.

She thought it was called the Davidson Building, but she had never been in it, certainly had never been behind it; she had no reason to come to such a place.

She was not in the habit of wandering into this part of the village. There was nothing down here but the mission, where she and Jimmie took their tourist friends, but it could be reached more easily by using Highway One. Besides the mission there was only a scattering of the uglier establishments necessary to a small town but kept apart, welding or the dry cleaning plant, various repair shops, warehouses, truck storage. The bus station was down here, and the train station. She did not frequent those places. Jimmie would be the first to tell her she had no business in that part of town.

I am Kate Osborne. I am the wife of Jimmie Osborne. Jimmie is the Beckwhite Agency manager and its top salesman. My husband is very well

*respected in Molena Point. He is a member of the
city council and he has been with Beckwhite's for
ten years. We have been married for nine years and
three weeks. We live at 27 Kirkman, seven blocks
above the village, in a yellow two-bedroom cottage
that cost Jimmie $450,000 four years ago during a
slack time in the real estate market, and would cost
twice that today. We shop for our clothes at Lord &
Taylor. Our house is beautifully decorated, just the
way I always dreamed I would make my home, and
we have a nice circle of friends, all professionals, all
excellent contacts.*

All, she thought, but one friend for laughs, one
disreputable bachelor who was anything but
upwardly mobile.

Clyde had begun as Jimmie's friend, but ended up
closer to her. She was more comfortable with Clyde
than with any of the couples she and Jimmie culti-
vated and, strangely, was more comfortable in
Clyde's ragtag house than in her own.

She had made their house beautiful for Jimmie.
Unwilling to hire a decorator, wanting it to be totally
hers, she had hunted a long time for the perfect soft,
cream-colored leather couches, for the handwoven
fabric on Jimmie's imported lounge chair. She had
hunted many galleries and decorator's showrooms
to find the five handmade, signed Timmerman rugs
for the living room. The sleek Boughman dining
room furniture had come straight from the factory.
Her signed Kaganoff place settings, arranged perfectly in the pecan china cabinet, had come from the
potter himself.

Strange that she could see the bright rooms so clearly, but when she tried to call forth Jimmie's face it was smeared and uncertain, almost like the face of a stranger.

She needed Jimmie. Right now, at this minute. She needed someone to help her. She was so shaky, felt far more disconnected from the world than when she woke sometimes in the small hours disoriented and terrified. As if she had been out of bed, out of the house. But of course she had dreamed that. Waking, she cowered away from Jimmie, frightened that she would wake him, frightened that he would see her so distraught.

Once when she woke up just before dawn, cold with fear for no reason, she had been shocked at the taste of blood in her mouth, so sharp and metallic a taste that she ran into the bathroom gagging—a taste as if she had eaten something unspeakably vile—and had thrown up into the commode.

Her only escape from those nighttime terrors, as well as from her recurring sense of confinement, was to walk the hills high above the village, to wander the steep winding lanes. Buffeted by the wind, standing in the cold, thrusting wind looking out at the sea and sky and the wide sweep of hills falling away below her, she could ease away those vague, invasive moments.

Alone among the hills she would feel peace descend, a quiet calm. Alone on the hills, she could be herself. And sometimes, up there on the hills, a delight filled her so intense it turned her wild—not a sexual wildness, but a longing to run, a strange and powerful urgency to leap away racing in the wind, free as some animal, wild and primitive, alive.

She could never explain those moments to Jimmie. The two times that she had tried, he was enraged. The second time, he slapped her. Almost as if he feared her joyous feelings, feared her happy, solitary rambles. As if he feared, most of all, her sense of freedom.

Had she been walking the hills when she found her way here into this alley? But why would she come here? There was nothing uplifting or exciting here. And why couldn't she remember?

Hesitantly she approached the gate, trying to avoid broken glass and filth beneath her bare feet.

With cold, clumsy fingers she lifted the latch and pushed the gate open.

The narrow street was flanked by eucalyptus trees; their scent, and the rattle of their leaves in the sea breeze tended, at once, to ease her anxiety.

To her left above the trees, and quite close, rose the tan stucco tower of the old mission. And she could smell bread baking; she turned, and recognized up the street the blue roof of Hoffman's Bakery. Yes, she was south of the village. She was on Valley Street, five blocks from the beach, but clear across the village from home.

She left the alley nervously, afraid she would be seen ragged and filthy. But, burning to get home, soon was running, and to hell with what people thought.

Just before Tarver Street she swerved to avoid a man leaving Mullen's Laundry. He stepped directly in front of her, and when she tried to go around he blocked her and grabbed her arm. She tried to jerk away; she started to shout for help, then thought she recognized him. He waited expectantly, as if she should know him.

Yes, it was Lee Wark, she knew him from the agency. Wark was a freelance car buyer—he furnished the agency with many of its used foreign cars.

What did he want with her? She tried to back away, but he held her arm tightly. His eyes frightened her. She wanted to cry out, but she couldn't seem to speak. When he didn't loose his grip she went limp, and stood relaxed, watching him, waiting for the moment she could jerk away and run.

He was wearing a tan windbreaker and a tan print shirt. His clothes were respectable enough, but his slouched shoulders dragged wrinkles into the jacket, making it hang like a rag. His long rough hair, and the thick, skin-colored salve he had on his face, made him look dirty. She felt trapped by his eyes, light brown eyes, small and unpleasant, no hint of human warmth. Still he hadn't spoken. She felt so cold, felt strange. She didn't understand what was happening. He had begun to whisper, words she couldn't make out, perhaps a foreign language, maybe his native Welsh. His unintelligable words terrified her; she jerked away, kicking at him. He grabbed her again. She hit him in the face and twisted, broke away and ran.

He shouted, pounding after her. She prayed for a

shop to duck into, but she was beside a tall, solid fence. She bolted for the shops ahead, but Wark grabbed her from behind, spinning her around to face him.

His voice was so low she had to strain to hear. But now she wanted to hear, suddenly she needed to hear, she longed to hear every whispered word. His words made a rhyme, soft and foreign and musical, words flowing all together. Sweet, so sweet, like music. His hands were huge. Immense hands jerking her up, dangling her off the ground. He was a giant swinging her in the air, throwing her soft furry body like a toy. She tried to scream and heard a cat screaming. She dug her claws into Wark's arm and leaped into his face, clawing and biting, wild with rage, hungry for the taste of his blood, relishing the feel of his tender flesh tearing under her claws.

He struck her. She fell twisting, hit the sidewalk on four paws running, dodging pedestrians' feet, running from him. Her vision filled with shoes and pant legs. She skidded past the wheels of parked cars and beneath bushes, then across a street. Huge cars exploded toward her; tires squealed as she fled between them.

The village she sped through was both familiar and totally foreign. She saw streets and buildings she recognized. But mostly she saw the bottoms of windows just above her, the thresholds of doors, saw feet and wheels and skirt bottoms. She dodged between potted trees, seeing little more than the pots, leaped beneath newspaper racks. The smells from the pavement were sharp, smells of people, of dogs. The sidewalks were so hard under her paws; every crack and pebble telegraphed itself through her body by way of her flying paws. She heard her pursuer pounding behind her. But his footsteps grew fainter.

When she at last reached home, she had lost him. Or he had simply stopped following. She didn't think until later that Wark already knew where she lived, that he had stopped by the house several times on business, once to consult Jimmie about a restored MG that Wark had bought for the agency.

Wark knew where she lived. He could find her any time.

Shivering, she crawled beneath the rhododendron bushes that edged the front lawn, the bushes she had so painstakingly planted, digging the deep holes herself, working in the peat moss and manure. Jimmie hated yard work.

Beneath her flowering bushes she lay licking the pain in her side where Wark had hit her. Slowly her breathing eased. She lifted an exploring paw and touched her long whiskers. What a strange, electrical sensation that made, the charge racing all through her. Her whiskers were little, stiff antennae sending intricate alarm messages through her entire body.

She flexed her claws, liking the feel of that, and she was amused to see Wark's blood on them. Casually she licked it off.

How sharp were the smells in the garden, the

spicy geranium, the bitter scent of the lantana growing along the sidewalk. Her ears flicked forward,
then back, catching each hint of sound. She could
hear clearly the sharp, bright, tin whistle call of a
wren several blocks away. She could hear the loud
rustle of a lizard across the yard, one that had got
itself trapped in a discarded candy wrapper.

Each sound was many-layered, not flat and muffled as it had come to her as a woman. Even the
breeze had far more tones than she had ever imagined, as did the pounding waves on the distant
shore.

For the first time in her life, her senses were totally
alive, as if she had just awakened from some som-
nambulant half-life. As she rose to prowl the garden, her pads telegraphed every turn of earth, every
degree of warmth or chill or dampness. Wandering,
she stared over her shoulder at her lashing tail, and
she liked the feel of that, too. Tail lashing seemed as
sexy and liberating as dancing.

She should have been terror-stricken at her transformation, should be screaming with horror, trying
to escape the thing she had become. Instead she felt
only delight.

For the first time in her life she was free. This
keen-sensed, sharp-clawed, soft-furred and perfect
creature was an entity all to herself.

She didn't need Jimmie. She didn't need any
human companionship. She didn't need money or
clothes or even a roof. She could hunt for her supper, sleep where she chose. She had no doubt of her
hunting powers, at the movement of each bird she

could feel her blood surge, feel her body and claws tense.

She had no need, now, of anything human. She was absolutely perfect, and free.

11

Night closed quickly around the Molena Point Library. From within, the bare black glass reflected walls of books; and striking through the reflections, shone the branches of oak trees which stood guard outside the Spanish-style building, big twisted trees sheltering the patio and the street.

In the library's reference room, Wilma turned off the computer and began to collect the scattered machine copies which were strewn across the table. Beside her, Clyde tamped a stack of papers to align the edges. They had been at their research, through the computers and books, since midmorning. Clyde now knew more about cats than he had wanted to know. The new knowledge was sharply unsettling.

Early that morning when he arrived at Wilma's house, she had just come in from looking for Dulcie, from wandering the streets and walking the shore calling the little tabby cat. He had set out with her again, working their way through the village, searching for both cats. Not until they returned to Wilma's kitchen to brew a pot of coffee, did he tell her about Joe's phone call.

Of course he had expected her to accuse him of a bad joke. But he had to talk about it, get it out. He had to bounce that unnerving call off someone: the rasping voice, the mysterious and knowledgeable presence of a supposedly feline communicator. What he badly needed was a dose of Wilma's sympathy and understanding. Maybe a dose of her more liberal outlook.

From the time he was eight, her supporting slant on the world had helped sort out his often confused views. His parents had been good and steady; but Wilma had supplied that extra something, had offered slants that sometimes were beyond the realm of parental conservatism. Wilma was able to see life with a rough, commonsense humor.

This morning, sitting in her bright kitchen, fortified with coffee and a slice of her homemade lemon cake, he had told her about Joe Grey's call, expecting—waiting warily for—the wisecracks.

But she did not accuse him of a bad joke. In fact, her reaction had been remarkable.

Wilma had reminded him that cats *were* strange. "That," she said, grinning at him, "is the very nature of cats."

"Hey, this is beyond strange. This is impossible."

Wilma shrugged, pushed back a strand of hair that lay tangled over her shoulder. "Cats' strange habits and strange perceptions, that's part of their charm. Read any cat magazine, look at the letters they receive from readers. Cats are admired for their peculiar behavior, their sometimes almost-human behavior."

She had recounted a dozen stories about the

strange deportment of individual cats. She told him about a cat who would lie beside the telephone recorder and punch the button to hear the little message his mistress had left. She told him about a cat who liked to unravel balls of yarn, and while doing so would weave the yarn around chair legs, back and forth into intricate and sophisticated patterns.

"That," Clyde said, "is not a normal cat."

"With cats, what's normal? You've read about cats who have wakened the family during a fire. And about the cats in San Francisco that alerted their households before the 1906 quake."

"But that's . . . "

"Of course a cat can feel the temblors long before people can. But, Clyde, it takes more than a dumb beast to want to alert his family. And what about the cat attack on a prowler? I read about that just a few months ago. Scratched the man so badly he ran out of the house, didn't steal a thing. And the cat that saved a baby from strangling by summoning the child's mother."

"They're all documented. As much as any report by a cat owner can be documented." She cut another slice of lemon cake for him, and filled his coffee cup.

"Look," he said, "this isn't just unusual behavior. Not like those examples. It's . . . "

"Impossible," she said, and shrugged. "What we need is more information. Before you think you've gone over the edge, let's see what we can find out."

He had not expected this reaction. He should have. Wilma was never one to let popular conceptions influence her. "And," she said, "if Joe Cat did phone you, if you aren't the butt of some joke—which of course is entirely possible—then maybe Joe's not alone."

"Not alone?"

"Why would he be the only cat with such talents?"

"Are you thinking of Dulcie? But she . . . "

"I don't know what I'm thinking. Let's go over to the library, see what we can learn. You're not going to find Joe until he wants to be found."

"But Dulcie hasn't come home, either."

"Let's go, Clyde. I worry about that cat too much. She's good at taking care of herself." She finished her coffee and cake, and rose.

Within ten minutes they were settled in the library reference room, and into the computer, pulling up references to cats in history, cats in folklore, cats in mythology. Within an hour they had begun to find unsettling references, tucked into more mundane material.

And then from the veterinary school at Davis they found several references to strange behavior in the feline.

Accessing the Internet, they printed out the pages. Wilma copied entries, as well, which were not strange in themselves but which might add to the overall picture. She was intrigued by articles on the building of the Panama Canal, when crates of alley cats had been imported by freighter to fight the overwhelming wharf rat population. She found similar references about the importation of stray cats to San Francisco during the gold rush, to control the rat infestation along the wharves. A local folklore of amazing cat stories had grown up, intertwined with gold rush tales.

Their research formed a disturbing fabric. Wilma was fascinated, as if their discoveries answered some urgent question of her own. He didn't realize the library was closing until the overhead lights began to go off, throwing the corners into darkness. "I thought they stayed open until nine."

"It is nine." She gave him an exhausted and satisfied smile, and began to collect their scattered copies. "I need a beer, I feel—shaky."

"I need three beers and a hamburger."

She brushed a fleck of computer paper from her sweatshirt. "Let's run by my place first. Just—to see if Dulcie's come home."

They retrieved Clyde's car from the library parking lot and swung by both houses. Neither Joe nor Dulcie had come home. Clyde fed his animals, and let them out for a few minutes, then they headed for Marlin's Grill. Driving slowly along the lit village streets past the few shops and galleries still open, past planters of flowers blooming beneath the reaching oaks, they watched for the two cats. Through the open car windows, the sea wind was damp and cool. They were quiet as they parked in front of Marlin's.

The grill's plain wood storefront made a stark contrast to the glittering glass and chrome high-tech gallery on its right, and to the used-brick building on the left, with its deep, flowered entry patio and exclusive decorator studio.

Marlin's Grill had no potted plants framing its door. No fresh, modern persona. It was dismally dated. Just a plain pine, 1950s exterior. And the interior was equally uninspired.

Marlin's was the product of a time when knotty pine paneling, inside and out, was big. The present management had seen no reason to change what had once been popular. Marlin's was possibly the only business establishment in Molena Point that was not regularly refurbished to a bright, exciting new interior. But who needed to redecorate, when the hamburgers were the best in town and the seven varieties of draft the best you could get anywhere on the coast.

Over the years, Marlin's yellow wood walls had darkened to the color of dead oak leaves. The leather upholstered booths were worn and cracked, but were deep, comfortable, and private. Clyde and Wilma sat at the back, away from the few other customers. They ordered an English dark draft, and rare burgers with onions and Roquefort.

When the Latin waiter had brought their beer and gone away, Wilma said, "Just before we left the library, when I went back to my office, Nina Lockhart told me that someone else has been interested in the material on cats."

"Oh? But not the kind of material we dug out."

"Exactly the same material. The same references."

Clyde watched her uneasily.

She said, "I remember the man, he came in late last week. I remember Nina helping him." She sipped her beer. "Nina pulled up the same entries we used. She brought him the same books." She set down her glass. "She plugged into the Internet, helped him copy the same pages we copied. I was working in a carrel across the room. I remember him because he seemed uncomfortable and hurried."

The soft overhead light brightened her steel-colored hair and the silver clip that held it. "He didn't notice me until around midmorning. But then, when he looked up and saw me, he looked shocked. Looked as if he knew me. He stared at me hard, then snatched up his copies and left."

Wilma sipped her beer. "He didn't finish copying the references Nina had set out, he just left."

"Who was he? Do you know him?"

"I've seen him around the village. I don't know who he is."

"He couldn't be an old parolee?"

"No." She laughed. "That man was never on my caseload."

"Did he check out books? His name would . . . "

"He didn't check out anything, just made copies. He didn't tell Nina his name, and he's not a regular patron. A thin man, tall and quite stooped. Light brown, straight hair down to his shoulders, muddy-looking eyes. Some kind of scars on his face and hands, covered over with flesh-colored makeup. Nina said it looked disgusting. He wore a tan windbreaker, tan cotton sport shirt, dirty white running shoes. Nina said he had a British accent. I could hear a little of it from where I sat. Lyrical—I'd say maybe Welsh—a poetic lilt. Charming, but amusing in such a dour man."

Clyde had set down his beer. "That was Lee Wark."

She waited.

"He's Welsh, been over here about ten years. A freelance used car agent. He deals with us, picks up special models for us across the country. Are you sure it was cats he was researching?"

"Of course it was cats. I told you, the same references we were using. What else do you know about him?"

"Not much. I think he grew up in a small fishing village on the Welsh coast. I get the impression his family didn't have much, that they were dirt-poor."

"Welsh," she said, making circles with her beer glass on the table. "The Welsh are raised on the old folktales, on Selkies, Bogey Beasts, the shapeshifting hounds."

The waiter brought their hamburgers. His English wasn't too good, he had trouble understanding that Clyde wanted mustard. He returned with catsup, Tabasco, steak sauce, and mustard, and seemed pleased with himself that he had covered all possibilities.

Clyde spread a thin layer of hot mustard on his French hamburger roll. "This is weird. Why the hell does Wark want to know about cats?"

Wilma shrugged, "I don't like coincidences. If Wark's connected with the agency, maybe I can learn something about him, some reason for him to be interested in cats, from Bernine Sage."

"I didn't know you and Bernine were friendly."

"We're not close friends, but she's useful. You've forgotten, we worked together in San Francisco."

He remembered then. Bernine had been a secretary in the U.S. Probation Office the five years Wilma was there. He wasn't fond of Bernine. She had been Beckwhite's secretary, and was the agency's head bookkeeper, a striking redhead who always dressed to the teeth, smart orange outfits, pale pink blazers. She was a woman who used the truth as it suited her, bending it for maximum advantage. At one time, Bernine had had a thing with Lee Wark. They had lived together during his swings through Molena Point.

Wilma finished her fries, drained her beer, and handed the briefcase across the table. They paid the bill and headed for her place, Clyde driving slowly, watching the streets. When he dropped her off, even before he pulled out of the drive he heard her calling Dulcie. His last view as he drove away was Wilma's thin figure in jeans and sweatshirt, standing alone in her yard calling her lost cat.

At home he dropped the briefcase on the couch and yelled for Joe. No response. He hadn't really expected any. He petted the dogs and the three cats, talked to them and gave them a snack. While the animals ate their treats he straightened their beds in the laundry room.

He had removed the door between the laundry and the kitchen, and had installed a narrow, two-bunk bed against the wall between where the washer and dryer stood and the corner. The dogs had the bottom mattress. The cats had the top; they could jump up onto the dryer, then onto their bunk, enjoying a private aerie that the dogs couldn't reach.

Both beds were covered with fitted sheets which could be easily laundered, and each bed had several cotton quilts that could be pawed into any required configuration. Finished with bed making, he popped a beer and went out to the backyard.

He called Joe, certain that the tomcat wasn't anywhere near. The stars looked very low, very large. The sea wind was soft; the distant surf pounded and hushed. The sound was steady, reassuring. He sat down on the back steps and thought about Joe Cat. He thought about the old Welsh tales, about cats which were more than cats.

He sat for a while staring at nothing, then drained his beer and went back in the house.

The three cats lay upon their bunk, the white cat's paw and muzzle draped over the side, looking down at him and purring. Rube and Barney were in their lower bed lying on their backs, all legs up, in a tangle of quilt. He rubbed their stomachs and said good-night, then poured a brandy and took Wilma's briefcase to bed.

Half-reluctantly, half-fascinated, he sat in bed sipping brandy and reading again the results of their search. Reading about hillside doors into unknown caverns, about strangers appearing suddenly in a small, isolated village. About the sudden appearance of dozens of cats in a little Italian town, as if from nowhere. He read about hidden doors into Egyptian tombs built for the exclusive use of cats. Doors to where? Why would a live cat need a door in a tomb?

Twice he got up, pulled on a robe he seldom

wore, and stood in the open front door calling Joe.
Three times he picked up the phone and listened for
the dial tone to be sure it was working. When he fell
asleep, with the light on, he slept badly.

12

 Kate gave a final lick to her paws and rolled over on the lawn in front of her house, letting her clean feet flop in the air above her, the fur bright now, and soft, a pale creamy shade.

The rest of her was still filthy. She couldn't bear to lick off all that dirt. She had clawed the worst of the caked mud from her tail but it still looked like a dirty rope. She rolled back and forth, trying to rub dirt off on the grass, then rose and checked the street for any sign of Lee Wark.

There was no one on the shady street. Beneath the oaks, only two cars were parked, both belonging to neighbors. When she was sure Wark hadn't followed her, she got up, stretched, and trotted around the side of the house and down the little walk between her flower beds. How strange that the yellow and orange flowers of her gazanias reached to her chin, and her irises towered above her.

Leaping to the back porch, she jumped up the screen door, snatching at the latch. She pulled and kicked until she had forced the screen open, and slid in between the screen and the solid door; the screen hit her hard on the backside.

Trapped between screen and door, she leaped again, gripping the knob between her paws, swinging boldly until it turned.

She was in, dropping down to the cool floor of her own bright kitchen.

The room seemed huge. The skylight rose incredibly high. Far above her, through its curved plastic, the late afternoon sun sent slanting shadows down her pale oak cabinets and yellow walls. Time to start dinner.

The thought hit her with a knee jerk reaction.

She lashed her tail, amused. From now on, Jimmie was fixing his own dinner.

But she guessed he had been fixing his meals—the kitchen stank of dirty dishes. She wondered how long she'd been gone.

Didn't he know how to rinse a dish, how to open the dishwasher? The floor tiles needed scrubbing, too. They were incredibly sticky. She sniffed at a spot of catsup near the refrigerator, and at a smear of jam. Every stain was magnified, both in smell and by her close proximity. People who owned cats ought to think how a dirty house looks to someone ten inches tall.

She had an unbroken view of the undersides of cabinets, and of the dust under the refrigerator. Far back beneath the stove lay the handle of a broken cup; she remembered throwing that cup in a fit of temper.

She had been alone. She hadn't thrown it at

Jimmie, though he had been the cause of her rage. She seldom let him see her anger, seldom let him know how he hurt her.

But that was past. Now, he could go torment some other woman.

When she leaped to the counter, her paws stuck in something he had spilled. It smelled like pickle juice. The sink was piled with dirty dishes. She stepped over egg-caked plates and pawed at the faucet handle until it released a drip of cold water. Hadn't he cooked anything but eggs? Maybe his cholesterol would do him in, and good riddance. She was thinking not at all like Kate Osborne.

Being a cat was more than liberating, it was salvation, a lovely reprieve.

She licked at the thin stream of running water until her thirst was slaked, then sniffed at her canning kettle, which Jimmie had dumped in the sink with dried applesauce clinging. There was no sign of the golden jars of applesauce that should be standing on the counter. She wondered if she'd already put them away. Or if Jimmie, in a fit of rage because she was gone, had thrown them out.

Well if he had, there was nothing she could do about it. Besides, cats didn't eat applesauce. Or, she supposed they didn't.

Though at the moment, it didn't sound bad. She was very hungry—she didn't know when she'd last eaten, but it felt like weeks. She wondered what she might have devoured beneath the wharf.

She pawed the bread box open but it was empty. She eyed the refrigerator, but gave that up. She certainly wasn't going to lick up dried egg from Jimmie's abandoned plates.

She leaped down, crossed the kitchen, and went to inspect the living room, amused by the wobbly feel of the thick Timmerman rugs under her paws. Their softness made her want to claw, but she didn't claw those lovely pieces. She scratched deep into the little Peruvian throw rug she kept before the front door to catch dirt. Raking long, sensual pulls at its center, she luxuriated in the delicious stretch of muscles down her legs and shoulders, the delightful stretch along her back.

She wandered the rooms aimlessly, looking up at the undersides of the furniture, and jumping up onto tables and onto the desk. She slid on her belly into the space beneath the couch, rolled over, and clawed a length of black dust cloth from the springs, then wondered why she'd done that.

In the center of the living room, on the slick oak floor, she chased her tail, spinning in circles, crashing into the rugs, giddy and laughing. She longed to race into the bedroom and stare into the mirror.

And she was terrified to look.

The idea of facing her own mirror and seeing it nearly blank, of looking into the glass where she combed her hair and put on lipstick, and seeing only a small cat looking back at her, was more than she could handle.

She delayed as long as she could, dawdling through the rooms, pawing at a loose fringe on the guest room rug, playing with a wadded-up scrap of paper Jimmie had dropped in the hall. But at last she padded into the bedroom and gathered herself, both in body and in mind, and leaped up onto the dresser facing her silver-framed mirror.

An incredibly ugly alley cat stared back at her.

Her color was the dirty gray of filthy scrub rags. Her fur was caked with dirt, her tail, that poor thin appendage looked, despite her efforts, like something that should be dropped in the trash. She was just a grimy cat skin stretched over thin, pitiful bones.

Standing on her dresser between her pretty, cut glass perfume bottle and her enameled powder box, a wailing mewl of rage escaped her. Sickened by the sight of herself, she began vehemently to wash, gagging at the taste of her dirty fur. She had to get the grime off, even if it made her throw up.

Licking, she could taste ancient fish on herself, and mud, and who knew what else. This was terrible, how did cats stand this?

But soon under her enraged washing her fur began to brighten, to grow lighter. A pretty creaminess began to appear, like the fur on her paws. And as her freshly washed fur began to dry, it began to fluff.

And she started to like the feel of licking, the feel of sucking away all the dirt. A surprising saliva came into her mouth, an aromatic spit that flowed sweet and cleansing, slicking into her fur and wiping away the filth, fluffing and brightening. Soon she was washing with a vengeance; she got so energetic about it that she nearly shoved her nice perfume bottle off the dresser.

As she removed the dirt she discovered little wounds, some quite sore, hidden beneath her fur, as if she had been fighting. Vaguely she remembered cat fights, brawling tangles, a lot of screaming and yowling. And for what? A rotten fish head or a patch of wet earth on which to curl up shivering.

Licking and salivating, drawing her tongue in long satisfying strokes, she was growing whiter. She had established a nice rhythm, pulling her barbed tongue down her sides and along her legs. Carefully and lovingly she groomed, attending to her pale, creamy chest, to her little, pink-skinned tummy, spitting on a paw to wash her face. It took a long time to get all her face and ears and the back of her head clean. The mirror was a great help, allowing her to check for missed spots. How could a cat wash properly without a mirror?

When she was satisfied with her face she reluctantly tended to her tail and to her hind parts, though she avoided certain areas. To lick herself there would take some getting used to.

It took a long time to clean herself up, but at last every inch shone creamy and fluffed. Staring into the glass at herself, she purred and posed. She turned around, gazing over her shoulder, vamping. She was the color of rich cream, her fur dense and short, as thick and soft as ermine. And her creamy coat was marbled all through with fascinating orange streaks, she had never seen a cat like herself. She looked as delicious as an exotic desert, like a rich vanilla mousse with orange marmalade folded in.

She was a big cat, rounded and voluptuous. The tip of her nose was shell pink, matching the translucent insides of her pink ears. Her eyes were huge and golden. When she opened them wide they were like twin moons.

Her creamy tail was fluffy now, and was delightfully ringed with orange, as if she wore wide golden tail bracelets. And when she smiled at herself, thinking giddily of the Cheshire cat, her teeth were very sharp, very white, as businesslike as her long, curving claws. How nice to flex her claws, to admire their sharp, curving blades. To think about them cutting deep into Lee Wark's soft flesh.

She grew nearly drunk with admiring herself and with considering the possibilities of this new body. What stopped this delightful adulation was that she stared at the bedside clock and realized it was after six, that Jimmie would be home. She was standing on the dresser twitching the end of her tail, wondering what to do, when she heard his car in the drive.

As she listened to the back door open and heard him cross the kitchen, she wondered what would happen if he found a cat in the house.

What would he do if he found himself alone in the house with a cat? If he were stalked through his own house by a snarling, predatory cat? She licked a whisker, playing over a variety of scenes.

But she had seen him throw rocks at dogs in the yard and smile when he hurt them. And once he had hit a cat on the highway but hadn't stopped—she had been unable to make him stop. She had come home weeping, had driven back there alone; she had searched for hours, until it grew dark, but she couldn't find it.

He was coming down the hall. His approaching footsteps sent a sudden terror through her. Chilled, she leaped off the dresser and dived under the bed.

Crouching deep under, in the faintly dusty dark, she watched his black oxfords move past the bed, heard him drop his keys on the dresser. In a moment he would dump his clothes on the chair, then get into the shower. She startled when he called her name. "Kate? Kate, are you here?"

Shocked, alarmed, she backed deeper under. Her backside hit the wall with a thump. Oh, God, had he heard her?

But it was only a soft thud. She stiffened when again he shouted.

"Kate! Are you home?"

But he was only calling the Kate he knew, as he called her every night. When he received no answer, he grunted with annoyance.

He hadn't taken off his clothes, hadn't gone into the shower. He sat down on the bed, creaking the springs, and she heard him pick up the phone. She listened with interest as he called the Blakes to see if they had any news of her. His effort made her feel better, as if maybe he did care.

He called the Harmons, the Owens, the Hanovers asking if they'd seen her yet. She didn't know whether to feel ashamed at the concern she was causing him, or to enjoy his distress. She listened with interest as he called Clyde.

He told Clyde she still hadn't come home, and

then he sympathized thinly with Clyde's own plight, which seemed to be that Clyde's cat was missing. Jimmie said that after all it was a tomcat, what did Clyde expect? The cat would come home when it couldn't screw anymore. He reminded Clyde that he, Jimmie, was missing his *wife,* not a cat. Clyde must have said something rude, because Jimmie snapped, "Maybe, but I doubt that!" and he hung up, banging the phone.

He made one more call.

Why would he call Sheril Beckwhite? She sat up straighter, hitting her head on the bedsprings.

But of course he would call Sheril, she was so recently widowed, she needed all the friends she could get. When Samuel was killed, everyone at the shop had rallied around to help her. Jimmie would be calling to help out in some way, do one of the little kindnesses. The fact that he was being extraordinarily thoughtful regarding Sheril did strike her. Jimmie didn't ordinarily go to any particular trouble over people.

But after all, Sheril had been his boss's wife.

When Sheril answered, Jimmie's voice was not that of a helpful friend. It was soft and intimate. Kate felt her claws reaching and retracting, felt her tail whipping against the carpet.

He told Sheril he would just get some fresh clothes and drop off his laundry, then he'd be over, that he'd pick up a couple of steaks and a bottle of brut.

Steaks? Brut? She didn't know whether to leap out and claw him, or to fall over laughing. Cheap

Sheril Beckwhite and dull, unimaginative Jimmie. That should be an exciting evening.

But how degrading that he had betrayed her with Sheril, of all the women they knew. Why Sheril? How perfectly ego-destroying.

Though in truth, she realized, she didn't give a damn. She wondered how long he'd been seeing Sheril. She was embarrassed that she hadn't guessed. Not a clue. How many people knew? How many people were laughing because she didn't know?

She wondered what Sheril was like in bed.

Maybe Sheril did things she didn't do, things that would shock Jimmie if she did them. The bitch syndrome. The good girl, bad girl syndrome. She had to stop her tail from lashing and thumping against the carpet; he was going to hear her.

She waited quietly until Jimmie had left the house—with his clean clothes and his laundry in two paper bags. Really classy. Then, frightened but resolute, she stood in the middle of the bedroom repeating the words Wark had whispered. She hardly thought it strange that she remembered them so clearly, they seemed seared in her head, as natural as, it seemed, was her ability to speak them. She didn't think, she just did it.

A sick feeling exploded inside her, a sick dizziness. But then a feeling of elation swept her, reeling and giddy; and she was tall again. Her hands shook. For a moment it was hard to walk, hard to remember how to move on two feet. It was very hard to turn and look into the mirror.

When she did look, Kate was there looking back

at her, tall and blond, the Kate she knew. How strange that she was cleaner; though her clothes were still a mess. She stood looking for some time, glad to see herself again.

It did occur to her to wonder which being she liked best. But what matter? She evidently had control of both. Talk about liberating.

She turned away from the mirror, and assembled her toothbrush and some makeup and toiletries. She packed panties and bras, a couple of blouses, a robe, stuffing everything into her overnighter. She tucked in an extra checkbook from her own account, then opened Jimmie's dresser and removed the stack of twenties and hundreds he kept for emergencies. She put the bills in her purse on the dresser.

She showered and washed her hair, gave it a few quick swipes with the blower and shook it into place. She put on fresh jeans and a clean shirt, and a decent pair of sandals. In the study she retrieved their savings book.

The balance was forty thousand and some change. She would stop at the bank and clean out the account before he found the book missing, open an account in her name alone. More than half of it was money her mother had left her. She figured she deserved the other half. She was straightening the pile of bank statements she had disturbed, when she uncovered, behind them, several small folders held together with a rubber band.

She removed them, frowning, and slipped off the rubber band. They looked like bankbooks, but she and Jimmie had no other accounts, just the one.

They were bankbooks. She opened one, then the next. All were on foreign accounts, two in the Bahamas, one in Curaçao, two in Panama. None was in Jimmie's name, but in the names of companies unfamiliar to her. The balances were all in the six figures, the largest for eight hundred thousand, none for less than three hundred thousand.

These had to belong to someone else. Why would Jimmie have them? Who would he be keeping bankbooks for? Her hands shook so hard she dropped the books. She knelt to pick them up, knelt on the rug staring dumbly at the evidence of accounts worth over two million dollars.

Maybe they were Beckwhite's. But why would Jimmie have Beckwhite's bankbooks, and after he was dead?

She thought of taking them with her, showing them to an attorney, or at least to Clyde. She started to put them in her pocket, but a coldness filled her.

If these were Beckwhite's bankbooks, what did that mean? And even if they were not Beckwhite's, if they were Jimmie's accounts, still, he was into something frightening.

She put them back in the drawer, and straightened the drawer, making sure everything was as she had found it. The bank statements had been facing with the cut edges of the envelopes to the back. The bankbooks had been facedown. Spines to the right? Or the left?

She was growing more shaken as the possibilities behind those huge accounts presented themselves.

She put their savings book back, too, just as she had found it. She didn't want him to know she'd been in this drawer; she'd rather do without the forty thousand.

She had meant to take her car, but she didn't want him to know she'd been home. She was, suddenly, afraid of Jimmie. She closed the drawer and left the room quickly.

In the bedroom she opened her purse and snatched out the twenties and hundreds, put them back in his dresser drawer. When she looked out the bedroom window to the backyard, she saw that the neighbors were setting up their barbecue. The afternoon had grown gray with cloud, heralding an early dark. In the Jenson yard, four tiki torches burned, and a crowd of kids had gathered. There were more than a dozen children in the yard. One of the Jenson kids must be having a birthday. She watched Joan Jenson spread a paper tablecloth over the long picnic table, watched the two Jenson boys weight down the corners with rocks. Well she wasn't going out that way in the form of Kate, not when Jimmie had alerted the whole neighborhood that she was missing. And when she looked out the front, there were cars pulling up in front of the Jensons'. She'd have to leave as the cat.

She stuffed her checkbook and keys in the pocket of her jeans. If her clothes had stayed with her, surviving the change, then whatever she put in her pockets might survive, too. She had no idea if there were rules to this alarming new life. She hid her purse and her packed bag on the shelf of her closet, behind some boxes. And she changed to cat with a haste that left no time to enjoy the strange rush it gave her.

The little cream-colored cat slipped out the back door, praying that the children wouldn't see her. Those boys were death on cats.

To leave without money or her car was going to present endless problems. But she couldn't shake the idea of getting out unseen. She wanted to leave no trail for Jimmie; not until she knew what was going on. Not until she knew where those bank accounts came from.

She fled around the side of the house and into a flower bed. She was crouched between some clumps of daylilies, looking out, scanning the street when a noise startled her.

Before she could run, Wark was on her, he had appeared out of nowhere. He grabbed her by the legs, squeezing with excruciating pain, and swung her high, then down toward the concrete. She fought, twisting, trying to reach him with her claws. A shout from the street put him off-balance.

But again he swung her.

This time she got a paw free and raked him. There was another shout, and she hit the concrete in a jarring explosion that dropped her into blackness.

The cat lay on the cement walk unmoving. Wark shoved her with his foot, pushing her under the bushes. Then, goaded by the shout, he ran, pounding away through the gloom that had gathered beneath the overhanging oaks.

Halfway down the block he swung into a black BMW and burned rubber, screeching away into the darkening evening.

13

Joe watched Dulcie remove every trace of fur from their freshly killed squirrel before she touched the rich, dark meat. He had watched her do this at each meal, remove feathers, claws, beaks; he had never seen a cat so fastidious. The squirrel was big and fat and it had fought hard, leaving a long bloody gash down Dulcie's leg. They had caught it by working together, by driving it away from all available trees.

He was impressed by Dulcie's bold hunting style. She was quick and fearless, and she could catch a bird on the wing, leaping to snatch it from the wind. He had seen her outrun a big rabbit, too, and bring it down screaming though the animal outweighed her. The rabbit had raked her badly. It hurt him to see her beautiful tabby coat torn and bloodied, hurt him to know how those gashes stung and throbbed. He had licked her wounds at intervals all night to ease the pain, and to prevent fever. She was so beautiful, so delicate. And so puzzling.

At first light yesterday morning he had watched her steal a child's blue sweater from a deserted porch. Waking, he had watched amazed as she dragged the sweater deep into the bushes.

Following her, he found her in a little clearing arranging the sweater, kneading and patting it. She was so engrossed she didn't hear as he brushed softly in through the foliage. When she had shaped the sweater to her liking she curled up on it and rolled onto her back, her head ducked down, her paws limply curled above her belly. Her purrs rumbled.

But when she glanced up and saw him she looked startled and embarrassed. And when he asked her what was so great about the sweater and why she had taken it, she clutched the blue wool with her claws and stared at him, hurt. He felt ashamed. Her need was a private thing, a preoccupation he should not have spied on and really didn't understand.

"It's so soft," she said, by way of explanation. "So soft and pretty, and it's the very color of a robin's egg. Can't you imagine wearing it, all soft wool against your bare skin?"

"I don't have bare skin," he said uneasily. What was this? What was she dreaming? What did she imagine?

"Don't you ever wonder, Joe, what that would be like? To be a human person?"

She had to be kidding. "No way. I may talk like a human and sometimes think like a human, but I'm a cat. I'm a fine and well-adjusted tomcat."

"But wouldn't you . . . ?"

"No. I wouldn't. I can just imagine it. Repairing the roof, mowing the lawn. Having to deal with car registration and income taxes. With traffic tickets and lawsuits and fixing the leaky plumbing." He shook his head. "No way would I be a human."

"But think about concerts and nice restaurants and beautiful clothes and jewelry. About being . . . I don't know. Driving a nice car, running up to San Francisco for the weekend." She stared at him, hurt.

When he didn't capitulate, didn't say it would be nice, she returned her attention to the blue sweater.

He hadn't meant to hurt her. In truth, her intense pleasure in the wooly sweater touched him, made him feel tender and protective. Made him very aware of her soft vulnerability. Made him smile, too. This was the same cat who had told him, late last night as they snuggled in the branches of an oak tree, how she had set out enraged to stalk the man who tried to poison her. The same cat who could explode into a hot chase after a wood rat, all claws and muscle, and nothing soft or helpless about her.

But yet the mystery was there, like another dimension behind her green eyes. And when she stood looking down the hills at the little village snuggled beside the wide sea, he knew she was not thinking cat thoughts. She was thinking of the tangle of human life; of the shoppers hurrying along the streets, the swiftly moving cars, the sounds of music and of human voices; of the richness of a world foreign to them.

He was hypnotized by her longing. And when, looking down at the village, she sensed him watching, she gave him a look so filled with mystery that it made his claws curl. And she laid her head against him, purring.

And in the night when he missed Clyde, and Dulcie missed Wilma, they would curl up close together and she would lick his face.

She told him a lot about Wilma, how they always shared supper, Dulcie sitting on a little rug by the sink, how they watched television curled on the couch together eating popcorn, and how nice it was to be in the garden with Wilma as she dug in the flowers; she told him about the books Wilma read aloud to her, and that was one thing they had in common, both their housemates read to them. The two humans shared a keen taste for mysteries, and traded paperbacks. They were always trading books, every time they got together.

But the biggest mystery, more urgent than any book, the real and frightening mystery, Dulcie found difficult to talk about. She would mention it, skirt around it, but soon change the subject.

And then on their third day in the hills as they crossed the yard of a redwood cottage where newspapers had blown out of the trash can, part of a headline drew Joe. He trotted over and found, on a crumpled portion of the paper, . . . POLICE SEARC . . . WEAPO . . .

He spread the paper out and smoothed it with his paw.

POLICE SEARCH FOR MISSING WEAPON

Police have as yet little evidence to the identity of the killer of Molena Point car dealer Samuel Beckwhite. No weapon has been found. Captain Harper requests that anyone having information about the killing, or anyone who may have found a heavy object such as a length of

metal discarded in the vicinity of Jolly's Deli, contact
him immediately. Employees of the Beckwhite
Automotive Agency have been questioned as a routine
matter. Captain Harper reminds Molena Point resi-
dents that witholding evidence to a crime is a felony
punishable by imprisonment.

"I don't understand," Dulcie said. "If the killer
went to the trouble of stealing that wrench from
Clyde, meaning for the police to find it with Clyde's
prints on it, why didn't he leave it beside the body?"

"I don't know. All I know is, if he plants the
weapon later, for the police to find, Clyde's in big
trouble."

"But why would he?" She cocked her head, puzzled. "Unless he means to use it to force Clyde to do
something."

"Or keep him from doing something," he said.
"All I know is, I'll feel better if—when we find the
damn thing."

But it was not until late that night after finding
the newspaper, that Dulcie woke mewling and shivering. Joe cuddled her close, clutching his paws
around her. "What is it? What's wrong?"

"I dreamed about the murder. I dreamed about
the third man."

"What third man?" he said sleepily, then woke
more fully. "What man?" He looked hard at her.
"There was no one else in the alley. Only Beckwhite
and the killer. And you and me."

"A third man." She shoved her nose against his
neck. "In the shadows. Standing near me between

the jasmine vine and a little oleander tree. When he saw the killer hit Beckwhite, he slipped away fast, down the dark street."

"Why didn't you tell me this before?"

"I didn't think of it. I supposed you saw him, too."

"What did he smell like? Could you see his face?"

"I couldn't smell anything, the jasmine was too strong. And it was so dark in the bushes. Just a darkly dressed figure, a thin figure, standing in the shadows where the bush and the vine blocked the light."

A tremble shook her, and she snuggled closer. "I saw the killer leap at you and swing his wrench. Then you ran, and a police light caught me in the face, I couldn't see where you went. I heard the police radio. When they shone their lights in, the killer moved toward me away from the street and stood still, his face turned toward me.

"He was looking right at me, Joe. He saw me, but then he turned back and chased you." She pressed her face harder against him. "He knows about us. He knows we saw—and more. He knows that we can tell what we saw."

She stared at him in the darkness. "I think that man knows more about us than we know about ourselves." And she curled down tight against him in a hard little ball.

He licked her face and ears. In a little while, he said, "If the second man was a witness, why hasn't he gone to the police?"

"I don't know. Maybe he's afraid."

"Or maybe he has other plans," Joe said. Then, "Maybe *he* found the wrench. Maybe he came back and found the wrench, before the police ever discovered the body. Maybe he's keeping it for his own reasons."

"Blackmail?"

"Maybe." He pawed at an itch on his shoulder. "Then again, maybe he didn't find it."

"Could it still be in the alley, somewhere the police didn't look? But how could the police miss it?"

"I don't know that, either. But it's a place to start looking. If it is hidden there, we need to find it before someone else does."

14

Twelve-year-old Marvin Semple had nearly finished his evening paper route. He was headed home on his bike, wheeling beneath low branches along the dim and shadowed residential street, pedaling past a row of overhanging oak trees, when he heard a cat scream.

The cry came from somewhere ahead, up near the end of the block. A second scream cut the silence, and he pedaled faster. Maybe a dog had some poor cat. He didn't know anyone on this street who had cats, but it could be any village cat. He was gazing ahead into the thickening shadows when he saw movement in the Osborne yard. A man was standing near the house straddle-legged, flinging something at the ground.

Crouching over his handlebars he raced toward the man, not wanting to believe what he saw.

Yes, it was a cat. The man was flinging a cat at the concrete walk. For an instant he saw the animal clearly, its pale fur bright in the dark evening as the man swung it down. Its scream chilled him. "Stop it!" What was the guy doing! Again the man flung the cat at the ground. Marvin shouted again and doubled over his bike pumping as hard as he could.

He screeched to a stop and dropped his bike, scattering his remaining papers as the man pushed the cat under the bushes. The guy ran. Marvin raced to where the cat lay.

Crouching, he lifted it gently from beneath the bushes.

It looked dead.

Holding it carefully, he glanced up in the direction the man had disappeared. A black car was pulling away fast, skidding around the corner.

He carried the cat beneath the streetlight and stood cradling it, trying to see if it was breathing. He couldn't see any rise and fall of its chest, but when he put his face to its nose, he could feel a faint breath. Gently he cradled it, deciding the best thing to do. The evening was fast growing dark. He was fifteen blocks from home.

Soon his exploring fingers found a barely discernible heartbeat. He could see no blood. The cat was beautiful, cream-colored and mottled with orange streaks. Marvin held her as delicately as he could in one arm. With his other hand he picked up his bike and straightened the nearly empty paper bags across the rack.

He laid the cat inside one bag, on a bed of folded newspapers, then removed the belt from his pants and used it to bind shut the bag against her escape. He knew from reading every book he could find about animals, that an injured cat or dog, or any injured animal, might run blindly away, evading the very person who sought to help it. If a horse or dog were injured, you should always get a lead on them to hold them steady. The first aid book said always confine a hurt animal as gently as you could. He had wanted to feel more carefully for broken bones, but he was afraid he'd injure the little cat. He picked up the scattered papers to balance the weight of the cat, so the bag wouldn't slide.

He was sure there would be enough air inside the closed canvas bag—he had left an inch hole at the top, and the canvas was thin and cheap.

With the cat safely bedded down, he took a running start and headed for the upper perimeter of the village.

It was six blocks to Ocean, then up Ocean five more blocks, then over two. He didn't know any faster way to get help. If he called his dad, it would take a while to find a phone, and a while more for his dad to reach him. And they'd still have to lift the cat into the car, and drive the same route he was taking.

He was headed for one of two animal clinics in town, the one his family used for their assorted pets, for their dogs and their guinea pigs and rabbit, the one he took stray cats to several times a month.

The clinic would be closed, but Dr. Firreti lived next door. Dad had gotten Firreti out of bed when their terrier was hit by a truck, and Firreti had been real nice. He'd saved Scooter. It had taken him half the night to patch up the little dog. Now, with this cat, Dr. Firreti wouldn't mind having his supper interrupted. Pumping hard, swerving around cars, Marvin sped the seven blocks to the blue frame house next door to the clinic.

He propped his bike against the porch, undid the canvas bag, and lifted out the unresisting cat.

Holding her close, he banged on Dr. Firreti's front door. Bending over her, he could still feel her breath soft against his cheek.

From inside he heard Dr. Firreti's step coming toward the door. Heard the knob turn.

The door opened and he looked up into the veterinarian's round, sunburned face. Dr. Firreti was silent and still for a moment. "Evening, Marvin. Good, another cat. How come it's not still in the cage? I see, it's too far gone to fight you. My God, we don't need a sick one."

"She's not sick. A man beat her. He banged her against the ground, tried to kill her."

Firreti bent down to look closer, touching the cat lightly, feeling its pulse, lifting an eyelid.

Marvin held her securely, in case she should come awake and try to get away. How many cats had he brought to Dr. Firreti? Nine, he thought. Nine cats, and with each one he had stood beside by the metal table watching Dr. Firreti prepare the needle—the syringe. And the last two times, Dr. Firreti had let him watch the operation.

Now, he was ashamed of his sudden tears. He hadn't cried with the other cats.

But then, no one had beaten them. No one had tried to knock the life out of them. And his dad said it was no crime to cry, not for something hurt and smaller than you. Not the way he'd cried for Scooter. But he was ashamed anyway.

"We'd better get her over to the clinic," Dr. Firreti said. He shut the door behind him, put a hand on Marvin's shoulder, and together they headed next door to the white, cement block building.

15

Pale fog brightened the midnight village with auras of diffused light gleaming around the streetlamps. The two cats ran through the mist like small, swift ghosts, hardly visible; it was a low fog, of the kind villagers called a marsh fog. Weaving near the ground it twisted in uneven masses along the sidewalks smearing the lit windows of the galleries, hiding the small details of doorknobs, hinges, potted trees. Above the low river of wet air, the roofs and treetops and the sky shone sharp and clear. The fog's white mass effectively veiled the brick alley beside Jolly's Deli.

The cats moved quickly into the alley past the fuzzed gleam that swam around the wrought-iron lantern. They stopped beneath the jasmine vine beside Jolly's back door, and looked back warily toward the street.

They saw no dark, moving shapes within the fuzzed light and mist. They heard no footfall, heard only the muffled beat of Dixieland jazz from Donnie's Lounge up on Junipero. The time was just after midnight.

Slowly and methodically they began to search the alley for the stolen wrench. They dug into the earth of the planters, around the roots of the oleander trees though surely the police had dug in the pots, looking for the murder weapon. The police must have investigated every crevice in the alley; but the cats searched anyway. Dulcie poked her paw into cracks beneath the uneven thresholds at the doors of the little shops, feeling into every small opening she could find in the old, renovated buildings.

They nosed up under the windowsills, and beneath the climbing vine at the other end of the alley where Dulcie had been crouching when Beckwhite was murdered. They climbed the jasmine trellis to the roof and searched there, pawing along the metal gutters into a sticky mixture of mud and slimy dead leaves. Joe grinned. If he found the mess repulsive, Dulcie was ready to retch. Every little while he heard her trying to lick off the stickly accumulation, then sputtering out cat spit.

They searched the entire roof, then searched the alley again, but they found no weapon.

Sitting on the damp brick walk, Dulcie said, "Maybe he still had the wrench when he chased you. Maybe he hid it somewhere else."

"If he just wanted to hide the evidence, it could be anywhere."

"But Joe, if he hid it to get Clyde—so if Clyde crossed him in some way, then . . . "

"I still don't get why Clyde would cross him. They weren't friends. It would have to be something at the shop." He frowned. "Clyde serviced the cars

Wark shipped in, but that's all. They didn't even like each other—at least Clyde doesn't much like Wark. What else could have been between them?"

She licked her paw. "Could Clyde know something about Wark? Something to do with the shop?"

Joe flicked an ear. "I've never heard him say anything. Never heard him say anything to Max Harper. If he knew something illegal that Wark had done, he'd tell the chief of police. Clyde's as straight as an old woman."

She shifted her bottom on the cold brick paving.

"But Clyde has been coming home from work really short-tempered lately. Not like himself. And when Beckwhite . . . "

He stopped speaking. His eyes widened. "I just remembered something." He spun around, and headed for the fog-muffled street. "Come on. Maybe I know where Wark hid the wrench."

She ran to catch up. Within minutes, racing along the foggy streets side by side, they slid into the crawl space beneath the antique shop where Joe had escaped from Wark.

The earth was cold beneath their paws. The dark, moldy dirt smelled sour. Neither of them mentioned the sharp scent of female cat. As they pushed underneath, festoons of cobwebs caught at their ears and whiskers.

He said, "That night, when I hid under here, just before I ran out the back, Wark knelt and looked in. I thought he meant to crawl in, but he only reached, feeling around. Maybe that's what he was doing; maybe he was hiding the wrench."

He reared up, sniffing at the top of the concrete foundation where it supported the heavy old floor joists.

Dulcie patted at the earth along the foundation beneath the opening, to see if Wark might have dug a shallow hole. But the earth was smooth and hard. Probably no one had dug in this ground for a hundred years, except for the resident cat—a female, she had noticed. She wondered about that, about why Joe had picked this particular building to hide under.

But he'd told her. It was the first place he could get under. All the other shops were store buildings on concrete slabs, no crawl space. This old place had been a house, once. Houses had crawl spaces. Wilma's house had a lovely crawl space, cool in hot weather, and delightfully mouse-scented, though the mice themselves had long ago met their maker.

She nosed along the top of the concrete foundation, reaching her paw warily behind ragged bits of black building paper. She didn't want to rip her soft pads on a hidden nail. She wondered how far Wark could have reached in. After some feet of poking and sniffing, she hissed, "Here. Something cold."

She pawed aside a ragged corner of building paper that was caught between a double joist. Its end sat securely atop the cement foundation, a double beam built to support some extra weight in the house above. Maybe a refrigerator; or more likely an old-fashioned icebox, from the age of the place.

The wrench was there, shoved up between the two joists. She tried to pry it out, then Joe tried, clutching it between his paws. The wrench wouldn't budge.

"Be careful," she said. "His fingerprints could be on it, as well as Clyde's."

"Damned hard to get it out without pawing. I wonder if he wore gloves."

"Well, did you see gloves on his hands?"

"I don't remember. I was too busy saving my neck. I don't know how else to get it down, without smearing it. Do you have a better idea?"

She stood on her hind legs, tapping at the wrench with a delicate paw. "What about this hole, here in the end?"

The small hole that ran through the end of the handle wasn't big enough to get a paw through. Joe could just hook his claws in. He pulled as hard as he dared without tearing out a claw, but the wrench remained solidly secured. As he backed away licking his paw, Dulcie said, "What would a human do?"

"How the hell do I know?"

He pictured with amusement Clyde's infrequent household repairs.

But Clyde did know how to use a lever. Clyde claimed levers had been one of the great steps forward for mankind. That seemed to Joe a little much, but what did he know? Certainly the lever system was innovative, at least from a cat's point of view. He'd been fascinated when Clyde levered up the heavy file cabinet in the spare bedroom, when a black widow spider ran underneath.

Clyde wouldn't have bothered to kill a spider just for himself. Probably if a black widow bit Clyde, it would be the one to die. But, afraid for the animals, he had lifted the file cabinet by wedging it up with a long metal rod. When the spider ran out, he stomped it. The smashed spider had left a permanent black spot on the carpet.

Thinking about the lever, he moved away into the blackness to prowl the cavernous space, and soon Dulcie joined him, searching for a piece of iron, maybe a scrap left from some repair, or even a stout stick to help dislodge the wrench.

Searching through the scent of female cat, he was interested that Dulcie did not remark upon the matter. Well if she wasn't asking, he wasn't offering. Anyway, what difference? That was another life. That female meant nothing, now.

When they found no lever to use on the wrench, nothing but a few rusty nails, Dulcie headed for the street. Trotting out the hole in the foundation, moving along through the fog, she stared up at each parked car until she found one with a window half-open.

She leaped, hung by her front paws, and climbed through, her belly dragging on the glass. She disappeared inside.

Joe waited, watching the street. Twice he leaped up the side of the car to stare in, but she was on the floor, he couldn't see what she was doing. When she appeared at the glass again, she had a thin, rusty screwdriver in her mouth, securely clamped between her teeth.

As she climbed out, the metal hit the glass with a little ping.

Within minutes, in the dark beneath the antique shop, they had pushed the screwdriver through the hole in the torque wrench. Bracing the lever against a joist, Joe laid his weight on the handle.

The wrench gave, it slid down a few inches.

But then it stuck again. He pried harder. He was able to force it slowly out, until it protruded so far he couldn't get a purchase.

When still it was stuck, Dulcie pushed him aside. Leaping up, wrapping all four paws around the screwdriver, hanging upside down, she swung hard, lashing her tail, jiggling and bouncing.

The wrench fell with Dulcie under it, she hit the ground hard. She lay still, panting. The wrench lay across her. Joe nosed at her, frightened, until she began to untangle herself.

"You okay?" he said at last.

"I'm fine." She licked at her shoulder. "We'd better find something to wrap the evidence. The police use plastic."

"Or we'd better wipe it clean, if Clyde's prints are on it."

"We don't know what's on it. The killer's prints could be there, too, if he was careless."

They found a newspaper on the porch of the antique shop and removed the plastic bag into which it had been inserted to protect it against damp weather. Within moments they had bagged the evidence.

They left the cellar carrying the heavy package between them, heading north. When a young couple approached them out of the fog, walking slowly

with their arms around each other, they ducked into
a doorway. When the bleary lights of a car sought
them, they crouched over the wrench to hide it.

Several times Joe left Dulcie guarding the plastic
bundle as he investigated possible hiding places. But
nosing through the mist into niches between walls
and into doorways, no place suited him. As they
approached the Dixieland music emanating from
Donnie's Lounge, he quickened his pace.

A walled patio served as entry to Donnie's neighborhood bar. The little stone paved rectangle was
bordered on three sides by wide flower beds planted
with marigolds. The flowers' sharp scent tickled the
cats' noses.

They laid the murder weapon among a tangle of
yellow blooms where the earth was soft, and they
dug.

As they loosened each flower, Dulcie laid it aside,
careful not to bite through the stem. She thought the
flowers might be poison, too. She had seen a list
once of plants poisonous to cats, but she didn't
remember much of it. Only oleander and, she
thought, tomato leaves. Who would want to chew
on a tomato vine? Each time the doors to Donnie's
swung open, the music burst out, hurting their ears,
but with a wildly compelling beat. The surge of jazz
was laced heavily with the sharp smell of beer and
whiskey. As they dug, Dulcie got that faraway look
as if dreaming again, dreaming about a night of
barhopping.

When the hole was some eighteen inches deep,
they lowered the plastic-wrapped evidence. Dulcie

said, "I feel like we're burying a corpse in one of those body bags."

"Should we say a few words over the deceased?"

She grinned. "Say a prayer for the man who killed Beckwhite. I think he's going to need it."

They pushed dirt back on top of the plastic-wrapped wrench, and Dulcie pressed each marigold in carefully, patting earth around its roots just as Wilma would do. "We don't want them to die, someone might investigate."

She resettled the last of the soil, then pawed dry leaves over the earth's wound. When no sign of digging remained, she stepped out of the flower bed, shook her paws, and licked the remaining earth from them. "No sense in leaving pawprints."

They were headed across the small stone patio for the street when the bar door swung open. Light from within hit the stone wall, driving them back down its length into shadow.

At first sight of the two men emerging, they hunched lower, and Joe swallowed back a snarl. Dulcie's fur bristled.

Lee Wark came down the path not five feet from them.

"And that's Jimmie Osborne," Joe breathed. "Why is Osborne out drinking with Beckwhite's killer?"

The men swung past them out the gate, both jingling car keys, and headed north. The cats followed, Dulcie proceeding warily, Joe pushing ahead quick and predatory, coldly hating Wark, and with precious little love for Osborne.

He'd never liked Osborne—the man was a bully and a coward. How many times when Jimmie and Kate were over to the house for supper, had Osborne been coldly rude to Kate.

Joe smiled. It made his night to annoy the man; he considered it a perfect evening when he could harass Osborne, torment him until he turned pale with rage. And with fear.

Now, hurrying through the fog after the two men, both cats grimaced at the smell of the killer. Wark's scent, more distinctive than Osborne's faint aroma, lingered sharply in the damp air. The smell goaded Dulcie, she forgot her earlier fear. Moving along beside Joe, she crouched to a slinking stalk, her ears clutched flat to her head, her tail lashing. Creeping through the fog, she gauged her distance. She considered the angle of thrust needed for a clean leap onto Wark's back, contemplating with delicious anticipation her claws digging in.

16

The cream-colored cat lay sick and confused, looking out through the wire door of a cage. Her thoughts were fuzzed, her vision blurred. She could make out rows of cages lining the small, square room, wire enclosures stacked three tiers high, marching around three walls. Nothing would stay in focus; no thought wanted to stay in focus. She lay sprawled on the metal cage floor, too weak to try to get up.

She was terribly thirsty. There was no water inside her enclosure, no small metal bowl as she could see in the other cages; she could smell the water, mixed with strong, less appealing smells. She didn't know how she had gotten into a cage; she had a sharp physical memory of Lee Wark throwing her against the concrete, a sharp replay of the pain, of terrible jolt exploding in blackness—then nothing.

She could remember waking before in this cage, waking then dropping back into sleep; her mind was filled with fragments of detached voices and with sounds that would not come together, with the rank medicine smell, and with the sounds of metal instruments against a metal table. She had no idea how long she had been here, no notion of time passing.

She remembered the feel of a plastic tube bound to her front leg, and of its little pin inserted with a sharp prick beneath her skin.

The stink of medicine clung to her fur. Her left foreleg was bandaged. It smelled so sharply of medicine that when she sniffed it she sneezed; the jolt of sneezing hurt her deep inside.

As her vision began to clear, she looked around intently for a way out. The walls behind the cages were made of unpainted concrete block. All but three of the cages were empty. The other tenants were a big brown dog sleeping deeply, four kittens asleep tangled together, and a black-and-white terrier pacing his enclosure dragging a stiff white leg. No, it was a white cast on his front leg.

Her eyes didn't work right, everything was fuzzy. Overhead, one soft light burned, a long fluorescent tube in a white metal fixture. Two other fixtures hung from the ceiling, one at either side, both unlit. The fourth wall of the room was blank except for a window and a metal-clad door, and a water hydrant protruding from the concrete floor.

The lone window was dark with night, but its blackness was rimed with fog, too, with a pale, blowing mist so thick that the window seemed to be underwater. The closed window was shielded from entry, or from escape, by a thick metal grid. As she looked, a flash of light ran striking across the fogged glass, as if from a car passing somewhere beyond; and she could hear the swift hush of tires on wet pavement, then the roar of several cars, fast-moving, as they would be passing on a highway. Her mind was as muzzy as her vision; but it clung to the one distressing fact that she was in an animal cage, that she was locked up in some kind of kennel.

But no, it was a clinic. Dr. Firreti's clinic. She had a vague memory of Firreti's face, round and smooth and sunburned, leaning close to her.

Firreti did something with stray cats. She could not remember what.

Why was *she* here? She wasn't a stray.

Had Lee Wark brought her here? Had Wark brought her here after he beat her? But why? For what purpose? Or had she gotten here somehow on her own after she was hurt, had come here needing help?

She stared at the closed wire door. Shut in like this, Wark or anyone could get at her. She tried to get up but lay back; the effort left her weak.

She could remember being in another room with concrete walls, and the same medicine smell; that was the room of the metal table and the voices, and the hands on her gentle but insistent. Her thoughts kept going around; she couldn't concentrate.

She tried again to get to her feet, but it was an effort even to lift her head and shoulders, a terrible effort to roll from her side onto her belly. When she did roll to that more erect position, pain shot through her ribs.

On the next try, she made it to her feet, but the hot jab forced her down again, crouching and panting.

She listened, but heard no sound from beyond

this room. She tried again to rise, suppressing a
sharp, involuntary mewl. She lurched up; and this
time she remained standing and moved to the cage
door, stood leaning against it.

The door was secured from outside. She thrust
her paw through, ignoring the hurt, feeling around
for a latch.

She found a slide bolt, and began to work at it,
pulling and wiggling it.

After a long time, when the bolt didn't give, she
forced both paws through. The pain as she stretched
out brought another involuntary mewl. The thought
of something broken in her small, tender self turned
her nearly helpless with fear.

But the thought of Wark finding her in here; or of
the veterinarian prodding and examining her fur-
ther, filled her with a deeper terror. What would a
veterinarian find if he studied her closely? Not a
normal cat. She fought the bolt, clawing and poking, bruising her paws, and at last managed to work
it free. The gate swung out so suddenly she nearly
fell.

Catching herself, backing away, she rested. She
had no strength. She was so terribly thirsty, panicked with thirst. The metal water pipe drew her
with an insistence that sent her leaping down; she
landed so hard on the concrete that tears spurted.
She crouched and threw up bile. The terrier began
to bark. His shrill cries filled the room, echoing,
hurting her ears.

Beneath the water hydrant beside a round metal
drain shone a small puddle of water. She lapped

thirstily. The floor smelled of Clorox and of dog urine. When the water was gone she fought to open the tap, but she couldn't budge it. Defeated, she approached the heavy door. The terrier's shrill staccato was so loud that it, too, seemed to be physical hurt.

Someone would hear him—there were houses close to the clinic. Staring up at his cage, she yowled at him. She might as well have yowled at a blank wall.

In desperation she shouted. "Stop it! Shut up and lie down!"

The human command, lashing out from a cat, threw the beast into a frenzy. Yapping he flung himself at his door, trying to get at her. As he heaved at the wire, she crouched before the tall metal door. Ignoring the furor she whispered, making the spell.

She was falling, spinning down, dizzy, whirling, then spinning up.

She was tall, she was Kate again. The terrier roared in shocked rage. She knelt by the hydrant, turned it on, and drank deeply, like a starving animal, getting soaked and not caring. Then, acompanied by the nerve-shattering barking, she turned the door's dead bolt and pulled the door open just enough to look out.

She was facing a parking lot, its black surface drowned by fog. She saw no cars—it was empty. The mist was penetrated by one dim light at the far corner. Up to her left was the highway, with its swiftly running smears of light.

Yes, this was Dr. Firreti's clinic. The front of the building would be to her left, facing Highway One.

Her pain was more tolerable now. Maybe, as a human, her sense of pain was duller, as were her other senses. But she ached all over. She longed for a nice hot bath, a hot supper, and a nice bed. She slipped out and shut the door.

There were plenty of motels nearby. She'd just check in somewhere, maybe order in a pizza. She grabbed at her pocket to see if she still had her checkbook.

Yes, it was still with her—so there were rules of some sort; but her credit cards were in her purse, on the top shelf of her closet. What would a motel clerk think if she walked in with no credit cards? Some motels wouldn't even rent a room if you didn't have a credit card. And she had no car, no luggage. She'd been so frantic to get out of the house, to get away from everything to do with Jimmie that she hadn't planned at all.

Why hadn't she had kept some of the money from Jimmie's dresser? She'd been stupid to put it all back. How would he know if she'd kept a couple of bills. She didn't even have any loose change for a phone call.

She could go home. No one would see her in the dark and fog. Unlikely that Jimmie was home, he'd still be in Sheril's bed. Go home, get her clothes and money and her car.

But she was afraid to go home, afraid of Jimmie finding her there; and she was ashamed of her fear.

She crossed the parking lot and headed down the

dim back street between fog-wreathed cottages. Only a few of the small houses had lights on behind the mist.

She had no notion what time it was. When she reached Ocean, the shops were closed, the streets were nearly empty except for a few parked cars. She turned away from the long block beside the automotive shop, and headed down into the village toward Binnie's. The little Italian restaurant stayed open late. They didn't have a pay phone, but they'd let her use the house phone. She hurried through the chill fog hoping a police car didn't come along and wonder about a woman out alone at this hour without a purse or coat. Hoping Jimmie wasn't cruising the streets looking for her. But fat chance of that, when he was playing games in Sheril Beckwhite's bed.

She couldn't leave it alone, the thought of Jimmie playing footsie in the conjugal bed of a dead man.

She could smell Binnie's garlic and spaghetti sauce before she reached the white-shingled, converted cottage. Gratefully she pushed into its warmth, in among the wooden booths and checkered tablecloths and the good smell of spices.

The café was nearly empty. There were only three customers, a young couple in the corner holding hands across the table like a couple in some fifties movie, and an elderly man in a dark suit, salt-and-pepper hair below his collar, sitting at the bar drinking espresso. He glanced at her without interest. She could see Binnie in the back, his dark, sleekly oiled hair, his long, solemn face above his white apron. He and the busboy were washing dishes.

She glanced through at them and waved, and picked up the phone; Binnie gave her a casual wave in return, nodding and smiling. Binnie's clock, behind the bar, said twelve-thirty.

She prayed Clyde would answer. Then she hoped he wouldn't. What was she going to say? Come get me because I can't go home? Take care of me because I have no home anymore and no money? Because I am a cat now, and have abandoned all human dignity?

The phone rang and rang.

Thank God he wasn't home. Oh, Clyde, please be home.

Maybe he had company, maybe he was not alone.

She had started to hang up when he answered. She clutched the phone. She didn't know what to say. She didn't know how to explain. It occurred to her that she could have walked down to his place, it wasn't that far. She felt as if, any minute, she was going to start bawling.

17

In the mist, the village was silent except for the muffled footfalls of the two men. Jimmie Osborne's oxfords pounded up the sidewalk but Wark's pace in his jogging shoes was almost silent; his soft walk made Joe's skin crawl. Following them, the cats drew closer, though Dulcie had restrained herself from launching in a clawed leap onto Wark's back. She moved quickly beside Joe, staying close to the shops where the fog was most concealing. Their quarry moved fast, jingling car keys.

The sour smell of liquor and cigarette smoke that clung to the men, absorbed while they sat in Donnie's bar, left a heavy trail behind them. Wark's voice was so soft the cats had to strain to hear. They caught a few indecipherable words, then Wark said, "No one'll link us to that."

"And the wrench?" Osborne said.

"It'll be found at the proper time. Don't fret." When Wark turned to look at Jimmie, his head in profile seemed unusually narrow; his nose protruded boldly. "Quit worryin', don't always be worryin'."

His low voice insinuated itself with an intimate penetration that made Joe shiver unpleasantly.

"You're sure Damen's prints are still on it?"

Wark's lilt sharpened with irritation. "They be on it. Quit fussin'. One phone call, the cops have the wrench and Damen's prints all over it."

"But all that handling, swinging it around while you chased the damned cat."

"Still had t'gloves on. Might be smearing it some, but it be full of prints, had t' be with Clyde using it every day. Back off, man. You be nervous as a cat your ownself."

"It's the damned cats that have me on edge. I didn't count on this when we . . . " He turned to look at Wark. "Where did the unnatural things come from? How do you think that makes me feel, my own wife . . . Did you take care of that?"

"I be workin' on it."

"You've had more than a week. You caught her once. Why didn't you . . . Now, who knows where she is?" He stopped to stare at Wark. "You're afraid of the damn things."

Dulcie had stopped, startled. She pressed against Joe's ear. "What's he talking about? What does he mean, about his wife?"

Joe thought about Kate Osborne, about her golden eyes that were not exactly like human eyes. He thought about the way she sometimes seemed to slip away within herself, dreaming—perhaps as a cat dreams private and delicious imaginings. He thought about Kate's catlike grace, about her easy, agile movements.

He thought about the time, when the two couples were in the backyard barbecuing, and he had trotted into the kitchen and found Kate alone, chewing on a raw steak bone. Clyde always cut the T-bone out before he grilled, he said you could plump up the meat better.

When Kate turned and saw him, her eyes widened. She had a speck of red meat on her cheek. She laid the bone down, embarrassed; then she seemed to laugh at herself. She knelt and picked him up, and tore off a morsel of the raw meat, offering it to him. "Hey, Joe Cat. What do you care what I eat?"

She put him down, and gave him another piece of steak. She left the raw bone on the paper wrapper on the counter, picked up her drink, and went back outside where the barbecue was smoking up the neighborhood.

Now, following the two men, he was quiet for so long that Dulcie said, "What? What are you thinking? Could Kate be . . . But that's impossible."

He thought about the rude way Jimmie treated cats and tried to avoid them. And about the rude, patronizing way he treated Kate.

This was incredible. Was he imagining this? Was he putting the wrong spin on the men's conversation?

Dulcie watched him with huge eyes, letting him work it out.

When he tried to imagine Kate Osborne as a cat, it wasn't hard to do. She would be a pale, voluptuous cat with golden eyes, very clean. He glanced at Dulcie and grinned. "Maybe," he said. "Maybe Kate is like us."

"I don't understand. How could she be? What— what would that make us? What . . . ?" She let her words trail off, her eyes huge.

"I don't know, Dulcie." A shock of fear had gripped him. He didn't like this. He'd just gotten used to a cataclysmic change in his life. He wasn't ready for anything more, not for the implications generated by this conversation.

But they had missed something up ahead; Jimmie had grabbed Wark by the shoulders.

"What did you tell her? What does she know?"

"Why would I be telling *her* anything?" Wark shrugged Jimmie's hands away, mumbling something they couldn't hear.

"She knows, doesn't she?" Jimmie growled. "That's why she ran away, she knows I want her dead. Well, you'd better do her, Wark. And soon. I don't like her roaming around loose. I wake up at night sweating. It's a nightmare that couldn't happen. I want it to stop happening.

"I wake up thinking it can't be happening, then I remember that cat you changed and killed. I remember how that cat looked." Jimmie shook Wark hard. "You'd better do her the same. And you'd better do those other two."

"Get your mind off t' cats. I be taking care of the cats."

"You haven't so far."

"I said, don't fret. I be doing it. And soon we be out of here, lapping up rum and playing with the girls, in Boca." Wark laughed. "But business first. We tend first to the job at hand. We've a long drive t'night. Might be we could tow one car, but I don't like . . . "

"Sheril's driving. I told you. It's not my fault your man got sick. Christ, he might have changed the VIN plate before he took off on you. I don't like doing that in the shop yard."

"We be back before daylight. T' tools all be there, only take a minute."

The two men stopped beside Jimmie's silver Bugatti; it waited low and sleek and bright, reeking of money. Joe had listened a dozen times to Jimmie's recitation of how fast the Bugatti was, how it could do over three hundred, and how much it would have cost if he hadn't got such a deal. Sure he got a deal. Five hundred thousand bucks worth of car, and Jimmie gave Kate the story that he got it cheap in a trade. He told Kate the Bugatti was a tax write-off, good advertising for the agency. Joe wondered how much Kate swallowed of that. Clyde said a hired salesman would play hell trying to take a write-off like that.

Jimmie said, "You better ditch the key, in case of trouble tonight."

"There won't be no trouble. Unless Sheril be messing us up. And who would know—innocent little brass key."

As Jimmie opened the driver's door and the interior light came on, the cats drew back behind a planter, jamming their rumps against a shop wall. Jimmie's face, lit by the low interior glow, appeared transformed, and not in a pleasant way. He slid into the low, sleek car. "Let's get rolling, pick up Sheril, or we won't be back before daylight." He stroked the pearly leather interior, and softly shut the door. In a second the Bugatti's engine came to life, a soft and powerful purr like a giant, sleek silver cat.

Wark moved on down the street to a black BMW. When, a minute later, his headlights came on, the cats shut their eyes so they wouldn't reflect. The cars swept by them and were gone.

And Joe crouched in the fog fearing for Kate. She had left home, run away. Was that what Jimmie meant? It was about time. He hoped she was a long way from Molena Point. He wondered if she did know what these two had in mind for her.

But if she didn't know, and if she was still in the village and she went home, if Jimmie found her there, that could be ugly.

Dulcie said, "Where are they going tonight? What are they up to?"

"They could be stealing cars. A VIN plate is an automotive identification." He slitted his eyes. "Is this why Wark killed Beckwhite? Were they stealing imported cars, and Beckwhite found out?"

"But they wouldn't kill him just over some cars."

"Expensive cars, Dulcie, if they're foreign makes. Cars worth way up in the six figures."

"Should we call the police? You could . . . "

"And tell them what? We're only guessing. If the police went up to the agency tonight, and nothing happened, then what?"

"We could go up to the shop. We could get inside and watch them."

He smiled. "I was thinking the same."

"But we have all night," she said, "and I'm done for. I need to rest and eat, first. We've been going since early morning."

"Okay. We'll try to find Kate, and warn her, then we'll grab a bite. I don't know where the Osbornes live. We need a phone book."

Dulcie stood still, watching him, the tip of her tail twitching. "I need to eat now." At his expression, she tightened her ears to her head. "We've had nothing to eat since early this morning, and hardly anything to drink—a few laps of gutter water. If you don't want a dead cat on your conscience, we'll eat first."

He rose and turned back the way they had come, toward the bar. "There'll be scraps at Donnie's, plenty of scraps. And they'll have a phone book."

She didn't move.

He stopped and looked back. "We'll just slip into Donnie's, find some leftover hamburger, and find Kate's phone number. They're so crowded no one will see us, just slip in between people's legs."

"Sure we will. And get stepped on or kicked trying to snatch a mustard-soaked bun or a few chips and peanuts and find a phone book." She sat down, staring at him.

"We need to find Kate, don't you understand. She's in danger, Dulcie. We need . . . "

She rose and started off up the street away from the bar. When he didn't follow she turned; her look seared him. "Come *on*, Joe. Wilma has a phone book. And there's food at home." And she trotted away through the fog, her ears and whiskers back and her tail lashing.

18

The bubble bath was scented with vetiver. The water was deliciously warm, easing every muscle. Kate lay back in the tub, letting her body relax, absorbing the welcome heat and sipping her cold beer, listening contentedly to the comforting sounds from the kitchen, where Clyde was cooking spaghetti for her.

What other man would rise from sleep at midnight, get dressed and in the car, pick her up and bring her home, then draw a bath for her and cook her supper? Above the herbal scent of the bubbles, she could smell the wonderful aroma of the rich sauce and garlic bread.

She had already consumed a plate of cheese and crackers, which he had set beside the tub with her beer. What a nice man he was, what an absolutely comforting and comfortable and caring man.

On the phone, when she called him from Binnie's, he hadn't asked one question. He hadn't even asked why she didn't just walk down to the house from Binnie's, it wasn't more than ten blocks. He had just come to get her, had walked her out and had sat in the car gently holding her, letting her cry.

Clyde might not have a lot of polish, he might make rude remarks, and belch with good-natured humor, but he was a veritable paragon among men.

He had not only drawn a bath for her and waited on her, he had cleared out the spare room as if she were royalty, had put fresh sheets on the guest bed, had hauled away stacks of tool catalogs and a pile of folded sweatshirts, had shoved the heavy, movable parts of his weight equipment out of her way, under the bed.

He had, while picking up his sweatshirts from the desk, quietly slipped a small spiral notebook and a thin briefcase in between two shirts, and carried them away.

Something obviously private; maybe something belonging to one of his girlfriends. She imagined that the vetiver bubble bath would belong to dark-haired Caroline Waith. Or maybe the little red-head—she couldn't keep them all straight.

She finished her beer, and lay back. She had remembered what it was about Dr. Firreti doing something with cats. It was, after all, nothing alarming. Quite the opposite. He collected stray cats from somewhere, very likely the thin cats under the wharf. Firreti neutered the cats, gave them shots, and turned them loose where they had been found. She grinned. That was what she had smelled in the damp sand, the metallic scent of a trap, mixed with human smell, probably Firreti's scent. Though it seemed more like that of a young boy.

She stepped out of the tub and toweled off, enjoying the thick, huge towel Clyde had provided.

Looking in the mirror, she studied with distaste the purple smudges across her body, like the marks of giant fingers. Ugly souvenirs of the bashing Wark had given her small cat self.

She resisted putting on Clyde's robe, though he had left it folded on the counter. She dressed in her jeans and shirt, and used his dryer on the edges of her hair. Then, limp and sleepy and content, she padded barefoot out to the kitchen.

Clyde turned from the sink. He was dressed in cutoffs and sandals and a faded purple T-shirt with a hole in the sleeve. He had set the kitchen table and was pouring her another beer. The fresh glass was white with frost from the freezer. She sat down at the table and petted the two old dogs who crowded against her knees.

But the three cats made no move to greet her. They sat in the center of the kitchen watching her intently, and not in a friendly way. She looked back at them uneasily.

She'd known these cats for years. They always ran right to her. All their lives she had held them and stroked them as they napped beside her or on her lap. She had played games with them, and had lain on the floor with all the cats asleep across her stomach.

But now, in those three pairs of eyes, was a look that chilled her. She daren't put out her hand and try to touch them.

Clyde seemed not to notice their wary behavior. Draining the spaghetti and pouring on sauce, he set the heaping plate before her. It looked so good she

wanted to push her face in, slurping. He brought a
bowl of salad and a basket of garlic bread, then found
the grated cheese and a bottle of salad dressing.

He sat down across from her, toying with his beer
and with a piece of garlic bread. She couldn't help
gobbling. She couldn't take time to wind her
spaghetti, she hardly cut it before she raked it in;
she was almost panicked with hunger. Clyde busied
himself with his bread and beer.

He not only ignored her unusual bad manners,
but waited patiently, without questions, for her to
explain her seeming abandonment to the streets
without money or her purse, without her car.

When, halfway through her meal the first empti-
ness was satisfied, when the good hot spaghetti
began to give back to her some warmth, she settled
back and slowed that flying fork. Sipping her cold
beer, she told the story slowly. She told him how she
had found herself in the alley behind that old office
building, standing barefoot among garbage, her
clothes and hands filthy, and with no memory of
going there, no idea of where she had been, no
memory of leaving the house. She told him how,
when she left the alley, Wark had chased her. She
told him what happened when Wark's foreign,
rhythmic words touched her. She told him how it
felt to be suddenly small and four-footed, how nice
her soft fur had felt, how nice it felt to run so swiftly
and to lash her tail. When he didn't laugh, she
described all the sensations she had encountered. She
was telling him what she could remember about living under the wharf, when he came to life suddenly.

"Stop it, Kate! For Christ sake, stop it!"

She stared at him.

"Why, Kate? Why would you make fun of me? And how did you know?"

She wasn't tracking, she'd lost something here. What was he talking about? "How did I know what? I'm not making fun of you." She stared at him, perplexed.

"How did you find out what happened? No one would . . . Did Wilma tell you?" He stared hard at her. "That couldn't have been you on the phone." His look bored in, then he shook his head. "No, not that voice."

She didn't know what this was about. He was so angry the look on his face made her cringe. She rose and went around the table, clutched his shoulders. "What's the matter? What's happened? I don't understand." She could read nothing from his expression.

They were silent for a long time, looking at each other, each of them trying to fill in the blanks. A little heat of excitement shivered through her. She said, "Clyde, where is Joe?"

"He's gone, of course."

"What do you mean, of course?" Her pulse began to race.

"He disappeared a few days ago. I'm sure you know all about it. You know he hasn't been home. That he . . . " He stopped speaking.

"That he what?"

"That he's . . . That he's been in touch," Clyde said tightly.

"How do you mean, in touch?"

"Look, Kate, why go through all this? Why bother? You know all about this. Why hand me that long involved story about wharves and about Lee Wark chasing you. Why not just . . . "

"Been in touch how, Clyde?"

"The phone, damn it! You knew that."

It took her a while to work it out. She stared at Clyde and stared at the phone. She studied him again, then gulped back a laugh.

Joe Grey had phoned him.

Joe Cat was like herself. And he had figured out how to use the phone.

She collapsed in a fit of merriment that weakened her. Joe Grey had phoned him, had talked to Clyde. Joe Grey was more than a cat, he was like her. And the nervy little beast had had the balls to phone Clyde.

She could not get control of herself. She rocked with laughter. She was giddy, delirious with the knowledge that she was not alone. That she was not the only creature with these bizarre talents, that there was another like herself in the world.

Clyde's face was a mix of rage and confusion. "What the hell's wrong with you! After the story you just told about turning into a cat, where do you get off laughing?"

She stopped laughing and watched him quietly. "You don't believe what I told you."

"For Christ sake, Kate."

She played it back to him. "You truly believe that Joe Grey phoned you. But you don't believe what happened to me."

He just looked at her.

"I wasn't lying," she said softly. Clyde was the only person in the world she could talk to—it was shattering that he put her off like this. "I wasn't lying, I'll show you."

And she did the only thing she could do. She used the only rebuttal that he would understand. She said the words, felt the room twist and warp. She let him see her do it, she forced him to witness the whole fascinating transformation. She was suddenly small, standing on the linoleum looking up at him mewling, lifting a paw to touch his leg.

Clyde's face was white. He stared at her, then rose, pushing back his chair, and backed away from her toward the hall door.

She followed him, and wound around his ankles. She felt him shiver. She brushed her whiskers against his bare, hairy leg, and heard him groan with fear. She pressed closer to him, rubbing her face against his leg. She was terrifying him. How delicious. It served him right.

He backed away, snatched up his beer, fled away from her down the hall. She heard the bedroom door close.

The three cats had run into the laundry and leaped to their high bunk. Even the dogs were wary, pressing against the back door, their ears and tails down as if they'd been whipped. She hissed at them all, flicked her tail, and trotted away down the hall.

She sat down in front of Clyde's closed door and licked her paws, listening.

She heard him rustling some papers, and muttering. She heard him set down his beer glass, heard the springs squeak as if he had sat down on the bed. She began to feel sorry that she'd scared him.

Well what had she expected? That he'd be thrilled?

One thing sure, she wasn't going to get anywhere with him, as a cat. She said the words again, and returned to the Kate he knew. She knocked.

"Can I come in?"

"Go away. You can stay the night if you want, in the guest room, or you can go sleep in a tree."

"Please, Clyde."

When he didn't answer, she pushed the door open.

He was sitting on the bed holding a sheaf of papers. When she opened the door he'd been staring sickly at the threshold, expecting the cat. He stared up into her face, shocked, then watched her warily.

"Come on, Clyde, I'm still Kate. The cat is gone. What's to be upset about?" She sat down on the bed beside him. He winced and moved away.

"Hey, I don't have rabies. I'm just Kate. How else was I going to convince you?"

He remained mute.

"I really need you. I really need to talk." She moved away from him to the foot of the bed, and pulled her legs up under her. She stared at him until he looked back.

"I have something to tell you, something else, that hasn't anything to do with—with what I just did."

She looked at him pleadingly. "I've left Jimmie. Or, I am leaving him. I'll have to get my things."

He didn't seem surprised.

She gave him a cool, controlled look. "It's Sheril Beckwhite. Jimmie and Sheril Beckwhite. So damned shabby."

It was hard to talk when he just sat looking at her. She told him how cold Jimmie was in bed, how decorous and boring; how, if she could get Jimmie drunk enough he would make wild, delicious love to her but that didn't happen often, and the next morning he wouldn't look at her; for days he would be cold and silent, as if he was ashamed, as if she shouldn't have such feelings.

How ironic, she said, that he'd gone to Sheril Beckwhite.

"And once when we were out drinking and walked the village streets for hours laughing, looking in the shop windows, acting silly, he said, 'You love the night, Kate. You love the night better than the day,' and he looked at me so strangely. As if he knew something," she said uneasily. "As if he knew, a long time before I did."

Clyde set his beer down carefully on the night table. He looked at her and kept looking.

"What?" she said, watching him, puzzled. And then a shock of anger hit her. "You knew about them."

"I knew. I've known for months. I didn't . . . "

"You knew, and you didn't tell me." She stood up, holding herself tight. "I thought you were my friend. I just finished baring my whole damned life to you, I just told you the most intimate secrets of my life. I just *performed* the most intimate, shocking, personal act for you, and you . . . You knew all the time about Jimmie and that woman and you didn't tell me."

"Christ, Kate, how could I tell you. I wanted to tell you. But I thought . . . I thought I might make things worse. Men don't run to the wives of their friends with that kind of . . . Jimmie and I go clear back to grammar school."

"You and Jimmie are not friends, you don't even like Jimmie. You let me suffer, when I was trying to make things work, trying to overlook the painful things Jimmie said and did, when I thought it was all my fault. And all along he was fucking Sheril Beckwhite and you knew it."

She had been going to tell him about finding the foreign bank books. She had wanted to ask his advice, try to figure out together what Jimmie was into. She had been so sure she could trust Clyde, that they were friends and totally open with each other.

And, she thought, if he hadn't told her about Jimmie and Sheril, what else was he keeping to himself?

Could Clyde be part of whatever illegal business Jimmie was into? Was Clyde a part of that?

Was that why he'd kept quiet about Sheril? Because of secrets, because of what he and Jimmie were doing?

She turned away and left the room. She went into the guest room and shut the door. In a childish gesture she pushed the lock and propped the desk chair against the door. She stripped off her clothes and got into bed, lay curled with her arms around the pillow, lost and angry and alone.

19

Kate woke reluctantly. A heavy depression gripped her. She had no clue to its cause. She was not fully awake; she felt certain that the missing fact would make itself known the moment she came alive. The waiting revelation would, in just a moment now, sock her in the belly.

The impending weight was accompanied by a sense of helplessness, as if she would be able to do nothing whatever about the bad news. In one more minute she'd have to face some unavoidable irrevocable truth.

And it hit her. She came fully awake: she remembered her small cat self.

She remembered changing from woman to cat. Remembered doing that last night in front of Clyde, remembered rubbing against Clyde's ankles. Remembered his sick disgust.

She remembered that he knew about Jimmie and Sheril; and that he hadn't told her. That he had behaved with some kind of uncharacteristic loyalty to Jimmie, a loyalty he would never exhibit, normally, given his long-standing antipathy to Jimmie.

She stared around at Clyde's small, homely guest room; at the drawn blind awash with early light; at the scarred oak desk, the ugly green metal filing cabinet, the large black-and-chrome structure of his weight equipment, whose immovable part was fixed to the wall. The weights, she remembered, Clyde had shoved under the bed. On the dresser, the small digital clock said six-forty.

She could hear no sound in the house. She couldn't hear Clyde stirring, couldn't hear water running. There was no impatient shuffling from the kitchen, no scratching at the kitchen door as if the animals were wanting their breakfast. Maybe Clyde was walking the dogs or was out in the backyard with them. She unwrapped herself from the twisted covers and rose, stood naked looking into the mirror.

Her eyes were puffy. A dark bruise sliced across her neck. The bruises on her arms and body, like giant finger marks, seemed even darker. Her short, pale hair stuck up all on end.

She smelled coffee, then, as if it had just started to perk, and heard from the kitchen the metallic sound of the can opener. She heard Clyde's voice, low and irritable, then heard the dogs' toenails scratch the linoleum, scuffling, as if he had set down their food. She heard a cat mewl.

She didn't want to face Clyde this morning. She'd just dress and slip out, go away somewhere. Maybe around nine o'clock she'd call the shop, disguise her voice and ask for Jimmie. Then, assured that he was at work, she'd go home, throw her clothes in the car.

She guessed she'd left Clyde's robe in the bathroom. She pulled the sheet off the bed, wrapped it around herself, and headed down the hall to wash. She wished she had her toothbrush, wished she had her comb and lipstick. Passing the door to Clyde's bedroom, she stopped to look in.

Last night when he was so upset, why had he been sitting on his bed calmly reading a bunch of papers? The briefcase and notebook lay in plain sight on the dresser.

She could hear him in the kitchen talking to the animals. She slipped in, walked to the dresser, and flipped open the notebook.

The pages were filled with short entries listing foreign cars: the year, the make, then particulars as to model, color, type of upholstery and the various accessories. All were expensive models. Each entry listed a state and county, a licence number, then a date and the name and address of a Molena Point resident. That could be the purchaser. Twelve pages were filled. She put the notebook down, opened the briefcase, and drew out a stack of papers.

They were photocopies of book and magazine pages. All were articles about cats. She read quickly, at first amazed, and then eagerly as one would read a letter from home filled with welcome news.

She read until all sound from the kitchen ceased. She stuffed the papers back in the briefcase, laid the notebook on top as she had found it, and fled for the bathroom.

She turned on the shower and stepped into the welcome warmth and steam. Why did Clyde have all that amazing stuff about cats? Where had he gotten it? And why, if he'd read it, was he so upset with her last night?

He must be trying to find out about Joe Cat. In her own distress, she'd almost forgotten Joe. Clyde had gone to some trouble to put together that remarkable information. But if he'd read those amazing articles, he shouldn't have been so upset last night.

She got out of the shower, brushed her teeth with her finger and Clyde's toothpaste, and brushed her hair with his hairbrush. When she came out, glancing down the hall, she could see him in the bedroom standing at the dresser.

He was dressed to go out, wearing tan jeans, a dark polo shirt and an off-white linen jacket. As she stood looking, he slipped the little notebook into his jacket pocket.

He moved to the nightstand and picked up the phone, and she backed away into the guest room. Through her open door she listened to him punching in a number.

He didn't ask for anyone, he just started talking. "Can I meet with you this morning? Yes, two days ago." He listened, then said, "Don't do that. That could mess us up real bad."

He listened, then, "No, nothing. But I'm not done with it. It's the money . . . "

Then, "Yes." He laughed. "Ten minutes," he said softly. "Soon as I can get there."

She shut her door quietly, dropped the sheet, and pulled on her clothes. She heard him pass her door going down the hall, then heard the back door open, heard him talking to the dogs as if letting them in. Quickly she slipped out to the living room and out the front door.

In the carport she slid into the open Packard, thankful that he kept the top down most of the time. The bright red car was an antique, valuable and lovingly cared for, always clean and well polished. Well why not? The men at the shop kept it washed. Sitting in the front seat she took a deep breath, whispered, and in an instant she was little again, four-footed, her tail lashing with nerves.

She leaped onto the back of the seat, then down to the floor in the back; she did it all so fast she thought she was going to throw up. Crouching on the floor among a tangle of jogging shoes, automotive catalogs, rags, paperback mysteries, and what smelled like stale peanut butter, she heard the front door slam, heard his footsteps. She hoped he wouldn't throw anything heavy on top of her. She heard him calling Joe. After a long silence, he came into the carport.

Standing beside the car, he called Joe again, and waited, then grumbled something cross and slid in. As he started the engine and backed out, Kate smoothed her whiskers and stretched out behind his seat, hidden on the shadowed floor. Stifling an excited purr, she smiled. Wherever he was going, whomever he planned to meet, he was going to have company.

20

Dulcie led Joe a fast pace home through the misty night; crossing her own yard she wasted no time but bolted straight in through her cat door and made for the refrigerator.

Coming down the fog-shrouded street, sniffing on the damp air the distinctive scent of Wilma's garden, of the geraniums and lemon balm, she had streaked blindly on, skimming past the big old oak trees, racing across the fog-obscured lawns, then careening inside far ahead of Joe.

The intricately broken front of the charming stone cottage, the deep bay windows, and the incorporation of the two porches deep beneath the peaked roof lent the cottage a warm and cozy appeal. Wreathed in fog, the house, Joe thought, looked like a dwelling in one of Clyde's favorite Dean Koontz novels, a house both mysterious and welcoming.

He felt uneasy, though, coming inside in the middle of the night, when Wilma would be sleeping. The intrusion made him feel unpleasantly secretive and stealthy. He would rather have had his supper

at Donnie's Lounge cadging hamburger scraps, half-
deafened by Dixieland jazz among the feet of happy
drinkers.

He pushed into the dark kitchen behind Dulcie
and found her stretched out on the linoleum
between the dim counters and the refrigerator
beside an empty kibble bowl.

She was still munching. "Home," she whispered,
smiling. Her breath smelled of kibble.

"Thanks for leaving me some."

"That was just an appetizer. As soon as I digest
this, we'll have supper."

He sniffed the scent of wet tea bags and onions
that radiated from the trash; these were mixed with
the smell of floor wax and of a woman's faint perfume. "Will Wilma hear us?"

"The bedroom's at the far end of the hall. She
sleeps like a rock. I can lie down across her stomach
at night, and she doesn't wake up. Come on," she
said, getting up, yawning. "When I open the refrigerator, hold the door open."

Lightly she leaped to the counter and pressed her
front paws against the inside of the refrigerator handle. Bracing her hind paws against the edge of the
counter, she pushed.

The door flew open, and Joe pressed inside to
stop it from closing again. Leaning into the chilly
shelves, he smelled the mouthwatering scent of roast
chicken.

Together they hauled out a package wrapped in
the kind of white paper Jolly's Deli used. They
pawed the paper off, tearing it with their teeth, to

reveal a plump half chicken, its skin crisp and brown.

Joe braced the drumstick between his paws and tore off chunks of dark meat as Dulcie quickly stripped meat from the breast. Dulcie was way too hungry to think about manners. The notion that cats were dainty eaters was an amusing human myth, no less silly than *Sick as a cat*, or *Cat got your tongue*.

They cleaned every scrap from the bones of the chicken, then they liberated from the refrigerator a foil-wrapped cube of cheese, a plastic container of oyster stew, and a wedge of cream pie. Dulcie lifted the aluminum pie tin out with her teeth, smearing her nose with cream. Joe hadn't realized he was so hungry. But as soon as the rich supper settled in his stomach he began to feel sleepy, and to yawn. He didn't want to sleep. If they planned to break into the automotive shop before dawn, he didn't need to pass out in a heavy, postsupper stupor.

He cleaned pie from his whiskers as Dulcie lifted what trash she could manage up into the trash receptacle. They left the floor a mess, but who could help it? They were cats, not kitchen maids.

They retired to the living room, to the top of Wilma's desk, where Joe pawed open the phone book and committed to memory Kate's number.

The room was old and comfortable. A worn blue afghan was thrown over the arm of the needlepoint couch. The big rag rug was thick and hand-braided, the desk was a nice rich cherry piece, carved and well polished. "Wilma keeps talking about redecorating,"

Dulcie said. "She keeps collecting pictures of rooms she likes." She shrugged. "Maybe she will, maybe not." The painting over the fireplace was the best thing in the room, a loosely rendered, painterly study of Molena Point cottages as seen from the hills, lots of red rooftops tucked among rich greens, and a slash of blue at the bottom that was the sea.

Joe lifted the receiver by the cord, and punched in Kate's number. The phone rang for a long time. He gave up at last, and lifted the handset back. He hoped she had left the village, that she was safely away from Molena Point and out of Wark's and Jimmie's reach.

At the back of the phone book, in the yellow pages, he found the automotive shop. Then, in the map at the front that the phone company had furnished for newcomers, he located Haley Street. He wondered if the people who had put together the phone book would be pleased that a cat was using their map.

The automotive shop was a block off Highway One, at the corner of Haley and Ocean. He thought that was near the vet's where Clyde took him once a year to get poked with a very sharp needle. Now that he had a little say in the matter, now that he was totally his own person, he wouldn't be dragged back there so easily.

The desk clock said two-twenty as they snuggled down on Wilma's blue afghan, pawing it off the couch arm onto the seat, and into a comfortable nest. Dulcie yawned hugely and rolled over, wriggling deeper into the soft wool.

Joe rolled onto his back, and licked a bit of chicken that he had missed between his claws. "I want to be out of here by four, up and headed for the shop."

"I'll wake up," she said sleepily. "I always wake up." Four o'clock was the shank of the night, the mysterious roaming hour; the time when her active imagination could soar into moonlit dreams; and, when the mice and small, succulent creatures come out of their burrows.

The warmth of the afghan seeped into their tired bodies, easing their tense muscles. But as Joe was dropping off, he felt Dulcie shiver.

He lifted his heavy head. "What? What's the matter?"

"I'm going to slip into the bedroom for a minute, and curl up with Wilma. Just for a little while, to let her know I'm all right."

He flattened his ears, hissing.

"Why not? What harm can it do? She'll be so worried about me. I've been gone for days."

"She might be so worried she'll shut you in. Maybe shut us both in, and call Clyde. You can bet he's told Wilma I'm gone." He sat up, alarmed. "Who knows what he's told her. Maybe about my phone call."

Dulcie smiled, and yawned. "So? It wouldn't matter, she won't tell anyone." She raised her head, frowning. "Haven't you thought about going home?"

"Wark knows where I live—and where you live. Sure, I miss Clyde. But even if I could go home, everything would be different.

"Life at home couldn't ever be the same as it was. What would we do? Have a beer together? Brag to each other about our conquests? Two crusty bachelors sitting around the living room telling each other whoppers about our love lives?" He stretched out again, wriggling deeper into the afghan. "A few days of that, and we'd both end up in the funny farm."

"Couldn't you just be yourselves? Why do you have to even think about it?"

"Because I'm not myself anymore. Not my old self. Because cats don't talk to people. Because cats and people don't have conversations. On the phone, okay. That was an emergency. But not everyday talk."

"But I . . . "

"On the phone, Clyde wasn't *watching* me talk. To talk to him in person—no way. Think about it. That's more than I could handle. More than Clyde could handle."

"But I've always sort of talked to Wilma. Roll over to tell her I want petting, scrunch down when I don't feel good. I tell Wilma a lot of things. I don't see . . . "

"That's body language. Body language is natural. Petting and stroking, tail lashing and snarling and purring and rubbing against, those are normal talk. But a conversation in the English language, face-to-face talk about everyday trivia, about what to have for supper, what channel to watch—no way."

She sighed. "Maybe you're right." She rose, prepared to jump down.

"Dulcie, believe me. If you go in there now, we might never get out of here. Not in time to see what Wark and Jimmie are up to."

"I suppose," she said, and settled back beside him, into the warm nest. "But I hate knowing she's worried about me."

He put his paw around her, laying his front leg over her shoulder, and licked her ear. "Do you think I don't feel bad because Clyde's worrying?" He yawned. "Go to sleep, Dulcie. There's nothing we can do about it; they'll just have to worry." He gave her a final lick, a little squeeze, and in an instant he was asleep.

Dulcie lay awake a long time, listening to Joe's faint, tomcat snoring. She longed to pad into the bedroom and snuggle down with Wilma. She had slept with Wilma ever since she was a tiny kitten, when Wilma brought her home, separating her from her litter because the bigger kittens kept pushing her out and wouldn't let her eat. She had vague memories of fighting those bigger kittens, but she never won.

She had slept in a little box, lined with something soft. At night, Wilma put the box beside her pillow, and whenever Dulcie woke hungry, Wilma would rise and go out to the kitchen to warm some milk for her. It didn't taste like the regular bottled milk tasted, that they used now. She supposed it was kitten formula, like in the ads on TV.

When she was big enough so Wilma wouldn't roll on her and crush her, she'd slept right on Wilma's pillow snuggled against her shoulder, into Wilma's long hair.

That was when Wilma first started reading to her, when she was snuggled on the bed late at night with her head on Wilma's hair.

She thought warily about the morning to come, when they would break into the automotive agency. She was just as curious as Joe was, about what those men were up to. But she thought she was more scared than Joe.

She wasn't afraid of dogs or other cats, but people could frighten her; and the automotive shop looked to her, when she hunted near it along the side streets, like a huge prison.

The idea of getting trapped within those high walls, of being cornered there by Lee Wark, was not pleasant.

But they had to do it. This was the only way she knew to stop Wark from pursuing them. Get the goods on him. Somehow, get him arrested. Then maybe the police would figure out about the murder, too, and Wark would be locked up for good.

But she couldn't sleep for thinking of being trapped inside that huge building. She tried to purr to calm herself, but she could only stir a small, uncertain growl. And she didn't sleep—she lay awake until time to wake Joe.

21

The Molena Point Police Bureau was in the center of the village, occupying the south wing of the courthouse. It was, like many Molena Point business buildings, a Spanish-style stucco structure with a heavy, red tile roof. The tower of the courthouse rose above it to its right, its peaked red roof the tallest point in the village.

At the curb before the front, glass door into the police station, two patrol units were parked. Identical units filled the back parking lot behind the building. There was a small public parking area directly in front of the courthouse. There, Clyde snagged the last space, pulling his red Packard in next to a rusting Suburban. The morning sun was bright. The time was nine-fifteen. From the number of parked cars in the public lot and on the street, he guessed that court was in session.

He left the top down, checking to be sure he hadn't left anything of value on the seat or in the glove compartment. There was nothing valuable behind the seat, only old shoes and junk. Anything deposited back there was quickly mixed with the tangle, and might never be seen again. He kept the outside and the front seat of the car clean. The backseat was no-man's-land, but he hardly ever had more than one passenger. He swung out and headed across the parking lot to meet Max Harper.

Entering the glass door of the police station he passed the fingerprinting bay on his right, beside which stood a stack of boxes labeled *copy paper*. An office boy was loading the boxes onto a handtruck, three at a time. He saw Harper at the back of the big room, past a tangle of desks where officers, coming off duty, were doing their paperwork. Harper motioned him on back, and rose to fill two Styrofoam cups from the coffeemaker that stood on a table against the wall. Clyde eased back between the desks, stepping over several pairs of rubber boots and around crammed wastebaskets. Who knew why they needed rubber boots in this weather? He wasn't going to ask.

Max Harper was tall and lanky, his thin face prematurely wrinkled, his expression habitually bleak. Though he was no older than Clyde, he joked that he could pass for Clyde's father. They had worked together for two summers, when they were still in their teens, on a cattle ranch north of Salinas. And for several summers they had ridden bulls in the local rodeos, raising a lot of hell, drinking too much.

Clyde reached the back of the room. They talked for a few minutes, then he picked up his coffee and followed Max down the hall toward one of the three conference rooms, where they could speak privately.

In Clyde's parked car, the cream-colored cat leaped up to the back of the driver's seat and clung, crouching. Looking out past the windshield of the big open car, she watched Clyde head for the police station. She hadn't expected to see him going in there; she had imagined something quite different. She had imagined a clandestine meeting in a back booth of one of the darker bars, or perhaps two cars meeting outside the village on some lone strip of highway. When he disappeared inside, she jumped gingerly out of the car to the blacktop. The jolt hurt, but not as it had last night, when she woke in the vet's cage. She was convinced that there were no broken bones, but only trauma and deep bruises.

Trotting across the parking lot, she stood to the side of the glass front door, peering around the molding to look in.

The room was full of officers, most of them occupied at their desks. Near the front, behind an official-looking counter, two male and one female officer were bent over a book or ledger. She knew from Clyde that Captain Harper wanted to redesign the station, give the separate operations more privacy and security. But Molena Point's mayor was a hard man to deal with, stubborn and shortsighted. Though, from the talk she heard, the mayor was sure to be replaced, come the next election.

She could not see Clyde inside. She backed away

from the door and slipped into the bushes that flanked the solid brick wall of the building.

She waited a long time. A woman went in, but she seemed nervous and kept glancing at her feet. A young couple entered but he held the door for her. There was no way a cat could slip past him, unseen.

Finally two officers entered arguing, swinging the door wide and hurrying on in. She nipped in behind their heels and slid behind a stack of brown cartons.

Concealed, out of sight of the preoccupied day watch, she peered out across the floor, studying the tangle of feet and desks and wastebaskets. The metallic bark of the police radio was low, but jarring. She thought communications was in a room to the left. Now she spotted Clyde, she got just a glimpse of him at the back of the room. He was moving away down the hall beside a uniformed officer.

She thought his companion was Max Harper, but who could see much from this angle? Everything was desk legs, human feet in black regulation shoes, and wastebaskets. She studied the room, weighing her options.

She could make a dash between the desks, hoping the preoccupied officers wouldn't notice her. Or she could go around through the courthouse, and in through the back hall. She had used that route from the courthouse the last time she renewed her driver's license. She watched an office boy making his way toward her, pushing a metal handtruck. As he approached the boxes, she hunkered low.

He stooped right beside where she was hidden, not an arm's length from her, and began to load boxes. She crouched, waiting.

When he had loaded his truck and headed toward the back, she fell in behind him, following at his heels. The boy, intent on his cart and on avoiding the room's clutter, had no clue a cat was following. She stayed close, but he hadn't quite reached the hall when she felt eyes on her. Warily she glanced around.

Behind the nearest desk, an officer was watching her with a little twisted grin on his round face, and one eyebrow raised. He was young and pleasant-looking, pink-faced. Just the kind of man, she thought, who might pick a cat up and make a fuss over her. She didn't know whether to move on quickly, or to get out of there. She sure didn't want Clyde to see her.

At the next desk a dark-haired woman officer had stopped work, too, and was looking, a dimple playing at the corner of her mouth. In a minute the whole room would know a cat had sneaked in.

But both officers remained silent, glancing at each other amusedly. Maybe she was the best laugh they'd had that morning.

She daren't look behind her. Who knew how many cops, by now, were watching her four-footed progress? But maybe no one would feel the need to pet the nice kitty, or to chase her away. What had made her think she could walk past a bunch of cops without every eye on her? She held her breath, and moved on quickly.

Catching up to the boy, she pressed so close to his heels that his pant legs brushed her face. And then ahead she heard Clyde's voice coming from the last conference room.

She swerved away from her companion and slipped inside.

Clyde sat with his back to her, at a conference table. She nipped under a line of straight chairs that marched along the wall.

Max Harper stood beyond the table, copying something on the Xerox. She backed deeper into the shadows, watching his lean back, his long sun-weathered hands delicately flipping over each page of Clyde's notebook and placing it carefully in the machine.

When Harper finished, he handed the notebook across the table to Clyde. She felt deeply relieved that Clyde wasn't into this ugly business with Jimmie, that Clyde had come to Harper.

Clyde dropped the notebook in his pocket. "Could you get to those four before they're sold? While they're still in the shop?"

"I'll call San Francisco this morning, see if we can get a man down here. If we can make those four, we'll start contacting everyone on the list."

"You can't keep it in the department, to save time?"

"We can check out the VIN numbers, but we can't check for any change in the motor numbers. We need a man from the National Crime Information Bureau for that. They won't tell any-one—not even law enforcement—where the num-bers are on the various cars and models."

Harper grinned. "Just as well. Let that information leak out, and the punks start using acid on the motor numbers, and it all hits the fan."

Clyde said, "Can you give me a few more days before you contact them? Another week? I still think there's something more."

"If you had one shred of evidence, Clyde . . . " Harper leaned back, lit a cigarette. He exhaled such a heavy reef of smoke that she had to press her nose against her leg to keep from sneezing. "You know I need sufficient cause for the judge to give us a warrant. If you had some indication of hidden cash, of laundered money . . . "

A jolt shook her. Laundered money. As in foreign bank accounts.

Clyde shook his head. "I've searched Beckwhite's office. Nothing. Nothing in Osborne's office. But I still think I'm right, that there's a money trail."

She waited while they discussed a deadline for Clyde, settling on three days, and finished their coffee. She could hear no sound from the hall, except the police radio. When they began making small talk about Harper's horse, which he kept up the valley, she nipped out, careened down the hall into the adjoining hall and through the inner door to the courthouse.

Crouched in the courthouse hall behind a concrete cigarette stand, hating the stink of stale ashes, she waited until two secretaries entered the ladies' room. She slid in behind them; and in a booth, she changed to Kate.

She came out of the booth straightening her shirt. She checked her reflection in the mirror, smoothed her hair. She wished she had a comb and some lip-stick. She patted the checkbook and keys in her pocket, and stood staring at herself, thinking.

She could go back into the station now, as soon as Clyde left. See Max Harper, tell him about the foreign bankbooks. Take him home with her, get the evidence he wanted.

But probably Harper would have to ask her questions, and right now she didn't want to answer any questions. Who knew, maybe he'd need a search warrant to take the bankbooks, even if it was her house. She wished she knew more about the law. The bankbooks weren't hers—they were Jimmie's property.

Or were they community property? By being married to Jimmie, was she somehow involved in his crimes?

And if Harper's questions and police red tape slowed her, the whole thing could take hours. She didn't want to stay in Molena Point, even for a few hours. She needed to get away, as far away from Jimmie as she could, away from the village.

She left the ladies' room and stood looking out the glass courthouse doors at the bright morning. Clyde's car was gone, the parking space beside the Suburban was empty. The courthouse clock said nine-forty.

She could be home, get the bankbooks and her purse, stuff her clothes in the car, and be out of there by ten-thirty. Bring the bankbooks back to Harper, then leave town. Drive up to the city, get lost in San Francisco.

Excited, and scared, she swung out of the courthouse and headed home, walking fast, hoping no one she knew saw her. It hit her hard that she was finally leaving him, but that no matter where she went, Jimmie might find her.

22

The sea wind scudded around Wilma's ankles like a seeking animal racing along the wet shore. The dawn sky was gray, the sea was the color of old pewter. She walked quickly, skirting just above the white foam and kicking through thin sheets of water that crawled black and sleek up the sand. Thinking of Dulcie, she felt ridiculously hurt.

The little cat had come home late last night but she had left again without ever padding into the bedroom to greet her, she had simply eaten and gone away again.

Around three-thirty this morning a thud had woken her. She had lain listening, wondering if she had a burglar, if someone was in the house. She thought it wasn't the first thud she'd heard; but it took a lot to wake her. As she lay trying to decide whether to get up, she heard the soft thump of the cat door.

She had expected that Dulcie would eat her kibble, then come on into the bedroom and settle down. She waited for quite a while, then swung out of bed and went to the kitchen. Before she could switch on the light she slipped and nearly fell. Backing up, she stepped on something sharp, a tiny object that pierced her foot like a splinter.

She flipped the switch, and in the blaze of light she froze, puzzled.

Chicken bones and greasy food were smeared across the floor. From the trash can protruded the white paper wrapper from the roast chicken she had brought home from Jolly's. And when she looked more carefully into the garbage, there was the stripped chicken carcass, as well as a plastic container that had held some oyster stew, and an empty pie tin. Greasy pawprints were everywhere. She sat down at the kitchen table puzzled, and then amazed. Then shaking with uncontrolled laughter.

There were two sets of pawprints, of different sizes. Both trails led to the living room, and up onto the desk. There was a smear of cream pie on the phone, and pawprints all over the phone book. The book lay open to the map of Molena Point. She stood at the desk remembering vividly Clyde's description of Joe Grey's telephone style.

She found a stain of grease on the couch, too, and the blue afghan was matted into a round nest which, when she laid her hand in it, was still warm. She was amused, but she was hurt that Dulcie had been there and gone away without even coming into the bedroom for a pet; and she was embarrassed at her resentment. It was childish and was silly.

She stroked the afghan where cat hairs clung,

Dulcie's chocolate and peach hairs, and Joe's short gray hairs, sleek as silk. She should call Clyde later, at a decent hour, tell him Joe had been there. She sat stroking the afghan, trying to imagine how the two cats had opened the refrigerator. And she was caught again in the haze of childlike astonishment that had haunted her for days.

But she was frightened, too. She couldn't stop thinking about Lee Wark—Wark and his mysterious interest in cats. Something about the man troubled her deeply. She did not like the pattern which was taking shape.

She had gone back to bed at last, but she didn't sleep. She rose before six, made a cup of coffee, drank it restlessly, and left the house, needing to walk off the tangle of disturbing thoughts which had descended. Shake them off or try to make sense of them.

She was well beyond the village, now, where big older homes sat atop the low cliff, their lawns and gardens glistening with sea spray. At the front of most of the houses, a large and well-appointed glass room had been added. Or, in the newer homes, a big sunroom had been integrated into the original design. These provided warm retreats all year from the ever-present sea winds, but offered a wide view of the changing sea. She liked to glance in at the expensive wicker funishings, at the carefully tended houseplants and the bright fabrics.

Sometimes she thought she'd love a house out here, if she could afford it. But these beachfront houses ran up into six and seven figures. When a hard storm hit the coast, however, she was glad enough to have her snug stone cottage away from the worst of the blow. And this stretch of beach, open and windy, and busy with running dogs, was not a good place for cats. There wasn't much shelter here, away from trees and the concealing hills, not enough shelter for Dulcie from dogs or from people. *Nowhere to hide from Lee Wark,* she thought darkly.

It wasn't coincidence that Lee Wark had spent hours in the library, researching cats. She kept seeing his angry eyes that day, when he looked up and saw her. Why would he be so startled, and so angry?

He was angry because he knew she belonged with Dulcie. For reasons still unclear, he hated the little cat. Hated her enough to try to poison her. Oh, that poison came from Wark. She was convinced of it. She didn't much believe in coincidences.

Somehow, Wark had known where Dulcie lived; he must have been watching the house, so probably he had seen her, too. Very likely he saw her leave the night he poisoned Dulcie's food.

She had found the buried bowl in late afternoon, when she went out to work in the garden. Puzzled by the mysterious ravages to her pansies, she had dug into the flower bed to replant them. Her shovel hit the bowl, hard and ringing.

When she uncovered it, the salmon was still in the bowl, rotten and stinking. Its smell had gagged her. But there was another smell, too, like bitter almonds. She had shoved the whole mess into a plastic bag, grabbed her car keys, and taken it to the vet.

Jim Firreti was certain the smell was cyanide, but to make sure, he had sealed up the food, bowl and all, and sent it up to San Francisco for analysis.

It was then she realized how dangerous Lee Wark was, and knew that she had to find out more about him. Before she left Firreti's office she called Clyde and told him about the poison, then she phoned Bernine Sage and made a date for lunch. Bernine was the only person she knew who might give her a clearer picture of the Welshman.

She left Firreti's office promising to keep Dulcie in the house, but she had no intention of doing that. How could she? Nor did she need to. Who else but Dulcie would have buried that reeking mess? Dulcie knew very well about poison.

She just hoped Bernine Sage would give her a clearer picture of the man. Bernine had lived with Wark, she had to know something about him. One way or another, Wilma thought, lunch would be informative.

The Bakery Cafe had opened five years ago in an old house a block above the ocean, a gray shingle structure with a deep veranda, which was now furnished with small tables. On nice days the veranda tables were all taken before noon. When Wilma arrived at twelve they were full, but Bernine had snagged the last one. She was just sitting down, her red hair flaming like a beach fire above a pale pink blazer.

Bernine Sage was forty-three, a natural redhead who showed off her coloring with tangerine lipstick, orange sweaters, hot pink silk. Today's cool pink blazer topped a white T-shirt and jeans, and flat sandals. Bernine's face was thin, her smile quick, though it seldom touched her eyes. She was tall, five-eight, and imposing enough to work a room without ever moving from one spot.

Bernine had left the San Francisco Probation Office at age thirty-eight, with twenty years and a nice pension due her. In Molena Point she had taken a job as curator for the Sentina Gallery, then later had gone to work for Beckwhite. Bernine knew how to run an office smoothly, and Beckwhite had paid nearly twice what Sentina could afford. She was personable, polished, skilled. To Bernine, appearances were everything. And manipulating the facts to enhance her work and her life was as natural as breathing. They had shared a few laughs over Bernine's past untruths, though Wilma didn't go along with Bernine's philosophy.

They made small talk while they studied their menus. When they had ordered, Wilma kept up the pointless chatter for a respectable interlude before she asked Bernine about Lee Wark. She would have preferred to cut right to the bottom line, but anything direct made Bernine nervous. Bernine liked the oblique approach. After ten minutes of idle conversation, Wilma got around to computers, at which Bernine was a whiz, and then to discussing the on-line system at the library, and the recent addition of the Internet. At last she got around to Lee Wark. Maybe her approach wasn't smooth, but it did the job. "There was an interesting man in the library the other day using the computer, doing some kind of research. I think you may know him. Thin, one of those solemn, hungry, artistic-looking types." Artistic was not the way she thought of Wark. "He had a fascinating accent; I think he may be Welsh."

Bernine's green eyes went agreeable and expressionless. "That would be Lee Wark," she said pleasantly. "He sells cars to the agency. He's a freelance car buyer, travels all over. What kind of research could he be doing? Something about foreign cars?"

"I didn't help him. It was his accent that caught my attention. Didn't you date a car buyer for a while?"

Bernine waited a moment, assessing her. "I dated Wark, a few years back. He used to bring me cactus candy from New Mexico, pralines from Atlanta, stuff he bought in the airport gift shops." She laughed. "I broke it off, it got too fattening."

Wilma smiled. "You were bored with him?"

"Sometimes."

"I'm not sure I understand about the car buying. Can't the agency buy the used cars it needs locally, with so many foreign cars in the village?"

"Molena Point people don't buy as many new cars as you think. Many of the BMWs and Jags and Mercedeses you see were bought from us used. And remember, Beckwhite's doesn't serve just Molena Point. We do two-thirds of our business with Amber Beach customers and with people all up and down the coast."

"And Wark ships the cars to you?"

"He ships them by truck, or sometimes he trucks them himself. He has a couple of trucks and trailers, those long, open ramps that you run cars up on."

"Interesting work. I guess he does this full-time, travels and buys cars?"

Bernine watched her carefully. "Wark travels maybe nine months a year. What's this about, Wilma?"

"Idle curiosity." Wilma laughed, sipped her tea. "What does he do the rest of the year? Didn't you vacation with him?"

"I'm over twenty-one," she said defensively. Then, more pleasantly, "He has a place in the Bahamas. He—it's very nice, very tropical and pretty."

"Sounds like a perfect relationship. He's not here often enough to get tired of him, and he takes you to a nice vacation resort. What made you break off with him?" She paused while the waiter set down their order, a chicken sesame salad for Bernine, a small sauté of crab for herself. She knew she was pushing Bernine, but Bernine, for all her bristling, would give in, if one kept at her.

But now Bernine seemed wound tight. When the waiter had gone, she said, "If you'd tell me why you want to know . . . "

Wilma just looked at her.

Bernine sighed. "I broke it off because Wark

was—so strange. Maybe it was his Welsh upbringing." She sipped her water.

"Strange, how?"

"Whatever this is about, Wilma, I really don't mind talking about him. Why should I?" She widened her eyes a little. "But I wish you'd tell me."

"I would if I could, Bernine."

Bernine sighed more deeply. "He made me uncomfortable. I never told him why I didn't—why I ended it. He has some really weird ideas."

"Ideas like what?"

Bernine nibbled at her salad. "It sounds crazy."

"Try me."

"I wish you'd tell me what you're after. Are you doing some kind of investigative work?" Half the retired probation officers they knew did some private investigation.

"I'd be breaking a confidence, Bernine. I can only tell you it's important. What was it about Wark that put you off?"

"He . . . It was the cats."

"*Cats?*" Wilma swallowed back an excited little *bingo*. She tried to sound and to look puzzled. "Why would cats . . . " She shook her head as if not understanding. "Cats, as in house cats?"

"Yes, cats. He'd get on the subject of cats until I could scream, I got really bored with it. Sometimes he scared me, the things he said and did."

She tossed back her flaming mop of hair. "I don't much like cats, but he was . . . We'd be walking down the street, he'd see a cat. He'd stare at it. Right there on the street he'd sort of—stalk it.

Would look and look at it, follow it, stare at it, try to see its eyes."

"How very weird. Did he ever explain his actions?"

"When he did explain, his ideas made my skin crawl. Superstitious ideas. He was really afraid of them, fevered."

"It's a phobia," Wilma said. "Some people have a terrible fear of cats."

"With Lee, it's more than phobia. He has this idea that some cats are—I don't know. Possessed. He thinks that some cats can—that they have, like a human intelligence or something."

Wilma laughed and shook her head. "He sounds very strange. Where would he get such ideas?"

"I don't know. His family was full of those stories."

"Family stories," Wilma said. "And he grew up believing them?" Then, "How does he get along with the men in the shop? I don't imagine he talks to them about his fixation."

"I doubt it. I guess the men like him well enough."

"How about Beckwhite? Did they get along?"

Bernine's salad fork missed a beat. "They got along fine, as far as I know."

"I heard there was tension between Beckwhite and Wark, some difficulty."

Bernine's eyes turned steely, then softened. "There's always some little difference of opinion, that's human nature." Her smile didn't hide an almost-frightened look. "You can't work in an office without differences. What is this? What are you into?"

Wilma poured the last of her tea. "I wish I could

tell you. You know me, I'm incredibly curious." She looked at Bernine blandly.

The waiter took their plates, and offered the dessert menu. They ordered a flan to share. When he'd gone, Wilma asked her about procedures at the shop.

Bernine, looking resigned, gave her a concise rundown of the routine for the newly arrived cars. Each vehicle was cleaned in the work yard behind the main building. Trash and forgotten personal possessions were removed; the car was washed, the interior given a cursory vacuuming, then it was sent to Clyde Damen, for a tune-up, for any needed repairs or replacements, and for steam cleaning of the engine. The last operation was a final wash and wax, more careful cleaning of the interior, and touch up to any small mars in leather or paint: a final cosmetic detailing before the car went to the showroom. Beckwhite's handled Shelbys, Ferraris, Lamborghinis, the newly resurrected Bugattis, as well as Mercedeses and BMWs.

"They treat every one like a baby," Bernine said.

"Who does the original cleanup, when the cars are first brought in? Different employees?"

"Are you writing a book about shop management? Jimmie Osborne does the cleanup."

"Well he's a nice young man. We were on the city council together one year."

Bernine sighed again. "I have to run, my dear. It's nearly two, I have a hair appointment." She glanced at the bill, but Wilma picked it up.

When Bernine had gone, Wilma sat for a long while, wondering exactly why her questions had so harried Bernine. Wondering why Bernine had seemed afraid.

23

During the hours of darkness, the outer perimeters of Beckwhite Automotive Agency were well lit. The one-story stucco complex occupied nearly a full square block at the corner of Haley and Ocean. It stood three blocks above Binnie's Italian, and just across from a beautifully landscaped Ocean Avenue motel. Backing on Highway One, which gave it easy access to buyers arriving from other coastal towns, Beckwhite's occupied a prime location at the upper perimeter of the village shops.

The drive-in entry to the maintenance shop was on Ocean. The agency's showroom faced the side street, its brick parking area separated from the street by a wide strip of bird-of-paradise plants. In the predawn dark, they shone waxen in the strong glow of the security lights fixed to the side of the building.

The front of the building was primarily glass. The small portions of white stucco wall were freshly painted, below the slanted roof of curved red tile. Twin bougainvillea vines, heavy with bright orange blooms, flanked the glass entry. The streets were silent, no car moved on Haley or up Ocean. The time was four-forty. The two cats stood up on their hind legs beside a bougainvillea vine, their paws against the clean glass, looking in.

The showroom was immense. Its pale walls provided an effective and contrasting background for the six gleaming imported cars which stood bright as polished jewels within the enclosure. "That red car at the end," Joe said, "is a new Ferrari. Clyde was reading an article about the new model just the other day; he left the magazine open on the kitchen table. It called the car sensuous and artful." Joe grinned. "Those guys who write about cars really take this stuff seriously. Said the Ferrari was sleek and curvy and provocative."

"It is," she said, cutting him a sly glance. "How would it be to drive something that elegant? Or that little blue, open job, careening down the highway?"

"Yeah, right. With the wind whipping your ears down flat and tearing through your fur."

Far to their left was a closed door with a small, discreet sign which indicated that it led to the drive-through entry and the automotive shop. Straight ahead behind the sleek foreign cars, along the back wall, a row of open glass doors and glass partitions defined the sales offices. Each was furnished with a handsome ebony desk, an Oriental rug, and three soft, leather-upholstered easy chairs.

They had already circled the complex, trotting along the dark sidewalk, crouching against the building when the lights of the occasional car approached. They had climbed up onto the roof, as well, in order to see the entire layout.

Behind the main building was a large, enclosed work yard surrounded by secondary buildings, some of which were open sheds containing various pieces of unidentifiable equipment and a few cars in different states of beautification or repair. To the left of the yard, Clyde's repair shop was closed off by a wide metal door. At the end of the shop, facing the showroom, a second garage door led to the drive-through. This door was closed. And the drive itself was enclosed by two chain-link, padlocked gates.

The yard was completely shut away from the surrounding streets except for this fenced entry, and for a narrower passage at the back, a slim alley which was also secured by two locked, chain-link gates. That passage led through to a narrow parking strip facing Highway One. Both wire gates hugged the concrete paving, and their tops touched the roof of the walkway.

They had seen, as they circled the block, that other businesses backed up to the rear automotive buildings. The row of separate stores facing the highway included a hobby shop, a quick-stop grocery, a photo shop, a laundry, and a restaurant. The intruding passage ran between the restaurant and the photo shop. Joe knew that in the daytime, when the gates were unlocked, agency employees went regularly through from their work yard to the side door of Mom's Burgers for coffee breaks and lunch. Clyde usually had a late breakfast there, as did Jimmie Osborne. Midmorning breakfast at Mom's had been a ritual with Samuel Beckwhite.

Standing against the front glass studying the

showroom and the gleaming cars, they stiffened suddenly and ducked as a car turned onto Haley.

It was a wedge-shaped red sports car, long and low and sleek, and was running without lights, headed from the residential section toward Ocean. It turned right toward the automotive shop. Joe thought it might be a Lamborghini, an elegant Italian job that would mean really big bucks. "Get down. It's slowing."

They crouched behind the bougainvillea vine as the sleek vehicle slowed before the entrance, then moved on. Seconds later another car followed: Wark's black BMW, also unlit. Both cars cruised slowly past and turned onto Ocean toward the shop driveway. The instant they passed, Joe and Dulcie swarmed up the bougainvillea and onto the tile roof.

Trotting over the low peak, they crouched at the edge looking down on the lit inner courtyard. A tow truck was parked beside the repair shop, close against the wall, a gleaming tan vehicle with Beckwhite's logo on the side. Dulcie said, "Why do they need a tow truck, when these are all such expensive cars?"

"I guess any car can have a problem on the road, maybe a flat tire. Anyone can have a wreck." Both cars had pulled into the drive. Wark got out and unlocked the wire gates, then slid back into the driver's seat. The two cars pulled in, followed by a low yellow roadster also running dark. When the three were inside, Wark closed and locked both gates.

"I think that's an antique Corvette," Joe whispered.

"The yellow one?"

"Mmm. A collector's model." He was surprised at how much he'd picked up from Clyde, and from reading over Clyde's shoulder.

Yes, the red car was a Lamborghini, a vintage model. He recognized the hubcaps from pictures, and he could vaguely remember the names of some of the antique models, Miura, Espada, Islero, because the words appealed to him; he didn't know which model this was, but it was bucks, all right.

Jimmie Osborne got out of the Lamborghini, and a woman emerged from the Corvette, her long blond ponytail, secured high on her head, bouncing like a tassel. She wore skintight black jeans and a black lace blouse that left nothing whatever to the imagination.

Crouched at the edge of the roof, the cats watched Jimmie unlock the door into Clyde's shop and wheel out a metal cart, its shelves fitted with tools. Jimmie laid a folded paper drop cloth on the ground beside the Corvette, and Wark slid into the front seat.

There he scrunched down nearly on his back and placed his feet, clad in black running shoes, up on the car's windshield.

The cracking glass sounded sharp as a gunshot, and the windshield popped out. Jimmie removed it and laid it on the drop cloth as Wark pried at something on the dashboard.

"He's removing the VIN plate," Joe said. "The identification number, it's on a metal plate. They're stealing cars, all right. I wonder if Beckwhite knew."

"Does the agency sell those cars?"

Joe licked a whisker. "Clyde was talking about VIN numbers on the phone just . . . " he stared at her, his eyes round. "He was talking to someone about stolen cars just before Beckwhite was killed."

Her eyes grew wide. "You mean Clyde's part of this—this car ring?"

Joe shook his whiskers. "Not old Law-and-Order Damen. No way. I think maybe he suspects something—he's been really irritable, coming home from work. And he hasn't seen Jimmie and Kate much lately. And he's been keeping some kind of list in a little notebook."

"Could Jimmie and Wark have killed Beckwhite because he found out? How could he sell cars in his agency, and not know they were stolen?"

"I guess if Wark had false papers, they could make it look legit. They killed Beckwhite for some reason. There's a lot of money down there, I'd guess the Corvette way up in the six figures, and the Lamborghini more than that."

"Maybe that was why Wark hid the wrench. Because they thought Clyde knew something. Maybe Clyde was nosing around." She looked at him thoughtfully.

He tried to remember Clyde's phone conversations over the last weeks, but he'd had no reason to listen carefully. The usual banter with his women friends, a complaint to the cleaners for losing a button on his sport coat, a call to his accountant. Dull stuff. He flicked a whisker and hunched lower, watched with growing interest as the men worked on the Corvette. He hadn't pictured Wark as a careful person, but the man was careful now as he installed the new VIN number. "I expect they got that plate from a wrecking yard, from an old wrecked Corvette, same model, same year."

"How do you know so much?"

"From Clyde. And from the late shows. What do you watch, late at night?"

"Wilma reads to me. Or if we're watching TV, I'm looking at the clothes and the beautiful houses."

As, above them, the sky began to pale, they drew back away from the roof's edge. From down in the yard, if one of those three were to look up, they'd see two cats as stark against the sky as gargoyles on a gothic roof.

They watched Wark rivet a new metal strip to the dashboard, working as carefully as a surgeon, while Jimmie removed a new windshield from the backseat of the BMW.

When the men were ready to install the windshield, Wark squeezed cement from a tube, around the edge of the Corvette's window frame. The smell rose up to the cats, making their noses itch and their eyes blink. As the men set the windshield in place, Joe could see a heavy bulge, like a gun, in Wark's pocket. He didn't mention it to Dulcie. She'd been through enough with Wark's poison and Wark nearly pushing her off the cliff. Even if it was a gun, why make a big deal.

Dawn was pushing into brightness as Wark and Jimmie cleaned up the edges of the glass and cleaned the new windshield. Dulcie crept forward, flattened against the roof, staring over. "What's the woman doing, rooting around inside the yellow car?"

"Sheril. That's Sheril Beckwhite."

The blonde was leaning into the Corvette, feeling under the seat. She had been rummaging through the interiors of all three cars as the two men worked. She seemed to be filling a canvas tote bag. When she backed out of the Corvette, rear first in the tight black jeans, the bag was fat and heavy. She was barely out of the car when Wark snatched the bag from her and headed for the small gate that led to the restaurant.

"Where's he going? What's in there?"

"Come on," Joe said.

"But it's . . . "

"Shh. Come on." He backed away from the edge and led her across the roof until they were over the repair shop. The sky above them was bright with pale, swift running clouds.

Below them in the yard, Sheril put her arm around Jimmie. "I'm starving, lover. And I'm purely dead for sleep."

"We're almost done," Jimmie said. "You sure you didn't miss any? We'll leave the cars in the yard—Clyde's expecting a delivery."

She laughed.

"A legit delivery. Come on, Wark can stash the bundles, we'll get some breakfast and grab a couple hours' sleep."

"I don't want to go to my place. I can just feel the neighbors staring, and it's broad daylight." She had a whiney voice, as annoying as sand between a cat's claws.

Jimmie mumbled something the cats couldn't hear, and Sheril giggled.

Wark was unlocking the small gate. As he swung it back, he looked up toward the roof. The cats sucked down as flat as frogs mashed on a highway. He seemed to be staring straight at them.

But he hadn't seen them. He moved on away, through the gate into the narrow alley between the stores that faced Highway One. "Where's he going?" Dulcie said, creeping forward. "What's he up to?"

Joe stared down at the tow car parked below them, and leaped. Dulcie followed, they made two soft thumps on the metal top, and hit the concrete running. Wark had disappeared but he had left the gate ajar, maybe for a quick getaway.

"Hurry," Dulcie breathed, glancing toward the two figures beside Corvette, and they slid through the open gate into the alley.

They were facing an open door, a side door into the restaurant; they could smell stale grease and cigarette smoke. The room was dark, but large and chilly. Behind them in the yard they heard the big driveway gate being rolled back, and heard one of the cars start and head out. They slipped inside, to Mom's Burgers.

The restaurant was so black they couldn't see Wark. And they couldn't hear him, not a sound. Moving in away from the square of light provided by the open door, they hunched in the blackness against the wall.

Before them loomed an army of tables, their legs standing at attention on the dirty carpet. Chairs had been piled up on top, a second row of mute soldiers waiting for the carpet to be vacuumed. At the far end of the room near the floor, a faint light shone. It seemed to come from around a corner, and they heard a soft thud, then a door suck closed with a pneumatic wheeze.

They trotted on back between the table legs to a short hall where, halfway down, a strip of light shone beneath a closed door. "Men's room," Joe said. They could hear from inside, metal rubbing against metal. As they pressed against the door they heard a *thunk*. Then silence. Then, in a few minutes, a metallic click like the turn of a lock.

The light under the door went out. The hall dropped into blackness. They leaped away as the swinging door opened, emitting a suck of air.

Wark passed so close to them that they could have clawed his ankles to shreds. He was carrying the canvas bag, a pale smear against his dark pants; even in the blackness they could see that it hung limp and empty.

He swung out of the hall and across the restaurant. In a moment they heard the outer door close and the lock slide home. They were locked in.

They heard the wire gate slam, the click of the padlock. Dulcie shivered.

"So he locked the door. So let's see what he was doing in there."

They shouldered open the heavy pneumatic door. As they pushed into the dark room, a chill hit them. Their paws hit cold tile. The room echoed with the sound of the door closing behind them.

Joe leaped up the wall, and leaped again. On his third try his groping paw found the light switch and grabbed it, clawing.

Light blazed, shattering against the white tile walls, reflecting back and forth from the slick surfaces, nearly blinding them.

The small, white tiled room had one booth, a sink, and a urinal. It smelled of human bodily functions and of Lysol.

Though the room was cold, an even colder chill emanated from the ceiling, where a black hole gaped.

Above them in the white ceiling, two accoustical tiles had been removed, leaving a rectangular space maybe three feet across, and black as the inside of a locked car trunk. The missing tiles were not anywhere in the small bathroom. Looking up into the hole, they could see in its dark interior only the edge of a wooden beam, and a few taut metal rods, maybe part of the grid that held the ceiling tiles. Joe thought that an attic must run the full length of the store complex. It would be the logical place to hide something.

But Wark would have had to stand on the toilet, then hoist himself up onto the thin partition of the booth. And even if the partition would hold his weight, Joe could find no footprint on the toilet seat or on the top of the tank. There was no strong scent of Wark around those fixtures. "He sure didn't use the facilities."

Dulcie reared up to stare with curiosity at the urinal, then grimaced, realizing what it was. "He used this," she said with disgust. She leaped to the sink and dabbled her paws in the few drops of water that clung around the drain, then examined the rectangular mirror.

The glass was fixed solidly to the wall—it was not like the medicine cabinet at home. In fact, nothing in the room seemed movable, except the toilet tank top, and what could you hide there? The tank would be full of water.

Dulcie said, "I know I heard a key in a lock." But there was no lock. They were still standing on the sink, pawing at the mirror, when the door swung open behind them.

24

 The swinging door slammed open; the cats had no time to leap off the sink. Wark stood staring in, into the bright white glare of the men's room.

His muddy eyes glinted with rage. As he lunged at them, they exploded apart. Joe hit the floor. Dulcie leaped straight to the top of the booth, brushing past Wark's face; but she moved too late, the Welshman grabbed her. As he fought the brindle cat, Joe leaped at his head raking and snarling. This allowed Dulcie to twist free from Wark's hands; with one last rake of her claws she sprang away into the attic and disappeared within the black hole.

When she appeared again looking over, Wark had scrambled up onto the toilet seat. But Joe still clung to his neck; as the Welshman fought Joe with one hand he grabbed for Dulcie with the other. She fled again. Joe propelled off Wark's shoulder into the dark behind her but he was off-balance. He hit the side of the hole, scrabbling into the soft tiles, felt them tear under his weight. Wark's fingers closed on his leg. Joe twisted, bit the offending hand, and leaped upward with a force that carried him up into the blackness.

They fled away through the cavernous dark along the wooden beams, dodging the thin metal struts. They heard him climbing, heard the clang of the porcelain tank as his weight hit it, then a dry, tearing sound as tiles gave way beneath him.

Then a loud crack, a sharp indecipherable word, and the clattering of dislodged porcelain as Wark fell.

Cheered by Wark's mishap, they turned to look back and in the darkness, Dulcie smiled. "Good for him. I hope he broke a leg."

But in a moment they heard him step on the toilet seat again, and climb. They moved away quickly.

The attic was vast, its low, sloped roof receding into an endless tunnel of unrelenting night, the tangles of metal struts hindering any swift flight.

"This can't just be the attic over the stores," Joe said. "It's too big, it has to go on over those open sheds." And why not? The buildings were all attached.

They were headed deeper in, toward the area over Clyde's shop, when Dulcie stopped and turned back, and began pawing at something.

In a minute, she hissed, "Here! Come and look."

She stood looking down between two acoustical tiles, where a sliver of light squeezed through no thicker than a thread.

Digging, she tried to force her paw through. They dug together, and soon widened the crack until they could see, below them, rows of metal pipes. The air smelled of cleaning solvent and steam. The pipes were loaded with hanging clothes, all sheathed in plastic bags. They were pawing again, trying to get through, when they heard voices from below, from an unseen part of the room. A woman's voice approached. She said something about tags and numbers, then laughed. They backed away into the dark.

"There's another crack," Dulcie said, "near the men's room."

"Its too close. He'll be up here in a minute."

But all sounds from Wark had ceased. They dug at the new crack until a tile shifted. A two-inch space revealed an office below. A battered desk and chair stood directly below them, and, to the left, two metal file cabinets. Next to those was a whole wall full of cubbyhole shelves, crammed with papers. As they fought to dislodge the tile, their faces pressed close together, they heard the men's room door open, and heard a sharp clang of metal.

"What's he doing?" Dulcie breathed.

"Whatever he's doing, you can bet your fur booties he'll up here in a minute. Dig harder."

But then a rhythmic noise began, a sharp metallic *Click click click* rising up. "Extension ladder," Joe hissed.

They fled again, but their scrabbling feet knocked the tile loose behind them; they heard it fall down into the office. Dulcie paused, turning back. "We've time to get through, come on." But Wark was already up through the hole, his lit face pushing up. They sped away crashing into metal struts and through cobwebs, dragging cobwebs with them. Joe didn't like to think about being trapped up there with no way to get out.

But if the attic continued over the drive and over the showroom, maybe there would be a way out. They raced on, slowed by the struts, swerving and dodging as if in some fun house obstacle coarse—a fun house as seen in nightmare.

They had scrambled around a corner, they were halfway around the U-shaped building, over the repair shop, when a perpendicular wall stopped them. They slid to a halt. The attic ended.

They crept along the wall nosing and pawing at its base. It was solid, not a hole or a crack. And suddenly light burst across the attic from behind them.

The swinging beam of a flashlight sought them, burning a path through the dark. They crouched behind a beam, out of its range. On it came, picking out beams and struts above them, frosting the curtains of hanging cobwebs. It glanced over the top of the beam where they crouched, and went on, as frantically and uselessly they dug at the floor. And Wark crawled nearer, swinging his light back and forth, searching.

This floor wasn't soft under their claws, not like acoustical tiles; this ceiling over the shop was hard and unyielding. And again Wark's light swung close.

"He has a gun," Dulcie whispered, "I saw it earlier."

Joe glanced at her. "I didn't . . . " But from below in the shop came muffled voices and the clang of tools.

"Clyde's down there, I can hear him. They've started work. If I shout . . . "

"No! It'll bring his light." She dug harder, clawing at the dense Sheetrock. Below they heard an engine start. But even over that sound, Wark would hear them digging. He had drawn closer, and his angle of vision was steeper now. He could see partially behind the last beam. Dulcie had managed a shallow indentation in the Sheetrock when Wark's light found them, blinding them. They were trapped in light. A shot cracked through the attic, exploding with ragged flame as Joe lunged against her, knocking her away. And a second shot thundered.

25

Ten minutes after Kate Osborne left the courthouse tucking her shirt more securely into her jeans, the cream-colored cat entered the Osborne backyard.

She scanned the neighbors' windows, and when she thought she was unobserved, she leaped to the back porch. There she rubbed against the porch rail, surveying again the adjoining dwellings.

She would just slip in, change back to the Kate who was Jimmie's wife, grab the bankbooks, throw her clothes in the car, and get out.

When she was sure she was alone she clawed the door open, wondering, as she kicked at the molding, if she was leaving claw marks.

Inside, she prowled the house, wary and skittish. Though Jimmie's car wasn't in the drive, she couldn't shake the feeling that he'd appear and grab her—that he would handle her as viciously as Wark had done, bruising and injuring her; that Jimmie was fully capable of killing her, no matter what form she took.

Gentle Jimmie Osborne, the quintessential wimp. Maybe wimps, when they turned mean, were the most vicious of all.

When she was satisfed that the house was empty, she paused in the hall. She was starting to say the Welsh words that would change her when she heard his car in the drive.

She ran into the living room and leaped to the back of Jimmie's chair, digging in her claws. Peering out through the curtains, she was struck by sunlight careening off the hood of the silver Bugatti. The car glistened in sleek silver curves.

She hated that car. The damned machine had to be worth many times what Jimmie had admitted paying for it. She hated that he lied to her. The Bugatti seemed all of a sudden the symbol of everything ugly about Jimmie. When she saw Sheril getting out, a growl of rage rumbled and shook her.

They came up the steps snuggling and pawing each other. Jimmie had his hand under Sheril's blouse, but why bother? Everything Sheril had was right there in plain sight. That lace hid nothing; she might as well be wearing a plastic bag.

She didn't know whether to change to Kate and confront them, or to hide until they left. Hide, then get the bankbooks for Max Harper, and clear out.

Hiding seemed so cowardly.

But if she telegraphed her punches, if she confronted Jimmie, he might snatch the bankbooks and take off. She might be physically strong enough to keep him from taking them, and she might not.

As they opened the door she fled for the bedroom and under the bed, into her shoddy little hiding place.

Crouching on the carpet just beneath the box springs, she heard them coming down the hall. Their voices sounded flat and tired. Had they been partying in Sheril's bed the whole night?

Their shoes hushed on the carpet. Sheril's nasal voice rose flat and piercing. Jimmie laughed, and Sheril started to giggle. It was ten o'clock in the morning. Why wasn't Jimmie at work?

Sheril said, "Your house is so—*domestic,* lover. Just like your little housewife."

Jimmie chuckled. "What if the little housewife comes home?"

"*She* walked out on *you,* lover."

"You like doing it in her bed, don't you, baby? Like a bitch wetting on another's territory."

Her claws knifed into the carpet. Her tail struck so hard at the springs she thought they'd hear her. They came into the bedroom yawning. Sheril kicked off her sandals and sat down on the bed, then her feet disappeared upward and the springs creaked.

Jimmie kicked off his loafers, dropped his pants and hung them over the chair. His shorts came next. So much for preliminaries. She could hear Sheril wriggling around, undressing. Jimmie moved to the bed; the springs creaked heavily as he lay down. *This is disgusting.* She fought a powerful desire to leap on the bed and claw them.

"I don't see why we have to wait, lover. I don't see why we can't get the plane reservations in another name, and haul out of here. It will be so sunny in the Bahamas, so nice and warm. If Wark's arrested for Sam's death, or if Clyde is, what difference? The cops have nothing on you. Why do we have to hang around being so careful? I mean . . . "

"Give it a rest, Sheril. How do you think it would look if we ran out now? You really want to blow it."

"But we didn't do anything. Not to Samuel. Wark did that. And Sam . . . "

"I said, cool it. We're not going now. Forget it. You don't understand anything about what the cops think, what the cops might find out."

Under the bed, Dulcie smiled. He was incredibly nervous. She guessed Sheril didn't see how nervous, or didn't care.

The springs squeaked as if he had rolled over, then again as he reached for her. She thought that they really needed a new mattress, then was both appalled and amused that that had even occurred to her. The springs kept squeaking. To the accompaniment of grunts and moans, she crept out and fled for the study.

As she pawed open the desk drawer, she realized with alarm that Jimmie's car was blocking the garage, that she couldn't get her own car out.

She wasn't leaving again without it. She wanted her car and her clothes and everything she could load into the Chevy. She thought about taking Jimmie's car, but abandoned that. He might let her go without tracking her down, but he'd be after that car. He'd raise all kinds of hell to get the Bugatti back.

Clumsily she clawed out the foreign bankbooks and the savings book, pawing them onto the floor.

This wouldn't do, she couldn't carry all these in her mouth, and fetch her car keys and purse.

She listened, but heard only a low moan from the bedroom.

She didn't want to go back in that room, but it couldn't be helped. They might be there all day. She wasn't staying in the house listening to that for hours.

Quickly she changed to Kate.

This time, as she changed, she got a nice little rush that amused her, a surge of exhilaration like a stiff drink. She was tall again, and very grateful, now, for the dexterity of hands and fingers as she picked up the bankbooks and stuffed them in the pocket of her jeans.

She laid the bank statements back in the drawer and closed it softly, then moved back down the hall toward the bedroom.

They were still at it. When, standing against the wall, she glanced in, she could see Sheril's naked thighs. They were both turned away. She slipped in, snatched her purse and overnight bag from the closet, and dug Jimmie's keys from his pants pocket, muffling the jingle in her tight fist. She lifted the cash from his dresser drawer, too.

She left the house by the front door. Sliding into Jimmie's car she backed it out, and parked it at the curb. She'd like to ram it hard into a tree, but that wouldn't be smart. She pocketed his keys, backed her own car out of the garage, shut the garage door, and headed for the police station.

*   *   *

She entered the station from the courthouse, praying that Max Harper was there. She passed his empty desk, looked around the room for him, then went up to the front, to the counter.

He wasn't in. She talked to Lieutenant Brennan, a deep-jowled man, older than Kate, who looked like he'd been poured into his uniform as clay is poured into a heavy mold. Brennan wouldn't tell her where Harper was. He couldn't tell her when Harper would return. His attitude was unnecessarily formal and distant. He told her only that Harper was out on a call. She wondered if that was what the sirens had been about—she'd heard them east of the village as she was driving to the station.

She didn't want to give anyone but Max Harper the bank books. "I'm certain Captain Harper will want to talk with me. I have something for him that I can give only to him. A piece of evidence that I think he'll be pleased to have."

"I'm sorry, Mrs. Osborne. I have no idea when he'll be back. Whatever you want to give him will be perfectly safe with me. I can lock any evidence in the safe, if that will ease your mind."

"Can you reach him? On the radio?"

"He can't be disturbed. Those were his instructions."

She thought that part was probably a fabrication. How would an officer know, when he left the station, that something even more urgent might not turn up? "If you can get him on the radio," she said patiently, "let me talk to him for just a second. I'll tell him what I have, and then I'll stop bothering you."

Brennan just looked at her. She pressed in again, bullying him, making such a pest of herself that at last Brennan sighed, swung away to his desk, and got Harper on the radio.

The call changed Brennan's behavior. Within seconds, Captain Harper phoned her, on a private line which Brennan said she could take in the back, at Harper's desk. She had graduated from faceless civilian to someone Brennan paid attention to. Walking back to Harper's desk, she glanced innocently at the two officers who had watched her, a little while ago, trot past their desks in cream-colored fur behind the heels of the office clerk.

She picked up the phone at Harper's desk, standing away from the desk top so she wouldn't appear to be reading the stack of papers and scattered notes.

Harper's voice was strained and hurried. "You have some evidence to give me, Kate? For what? What kind of evidence? What is it that can't wait?" He did sound as if he was in the middle of something urgent.

"I have some bankbooks of Jimmie's. They were in our desk."

"What kind of bankbooks? Tell me about them." His voice had softened, and slowed. He sounded like he might be sitting down.

"There are five books, on five foreign accounts. Big balances. Several hundred thousand each. Money," she said, "that he couldn't have legally. I didn't know what else to do with them, but I think they're important. I didn't know who else to go to. I don't have an attorney, not one I trust."

She couldn't say that she knew Harper wanted the bankbooks, that she had heard him tell Clyde how important this evidence was. "There are two accounts in the Bahamas, two in Panama, one in Curaçao. The sums have been deposited over a four-year period. They add up to more than two million. This year's deposits are about two hundred and fifty thousand. Captain Harper, there's no way Jimmie could have this kind of money."

"Kate, you bet I want to see them. Can you wait at the station for, say, half an hour? We're in the middle of something urgent here, but I'll be back as soon as I can. Within the hour."

"I have some errands. Could I come where you are?"

"No. Will you leave the books at the station? Meet me there in an hour?"

"I'd rather give them to you."

"Kate, give them to Officer Brennan. He's completely reliable. Those bankbooks are—may be more important than you can guess. You can watch Brennan book them in, watch him put them in the safe. Tell him to make photocopies for you. And Kate, do you know where Jimmie is?"

"Right now? He's . . . at home. He's—in bed."

"At home? Is he sick?"

"He's—not alone."

"Oh?" There was a long pause, then, "Thank you, Kate. Let me talk to Brennan. I'll see you at the station in an hour. Meantime, be . . . Don't go home."

"Not likely," she said, laughing. But she felt, suddenly, chilled and shaky.

She nodded to Officer Brennan, and he picked up an extension. She hung up. Why had Harper asked her where Jimmie was? Why wouldn't he assume that Jimmie was at the shop?

In a minute Brennan hung up and came out to the back, his stomach preceding him slightly in the tight shirt. He led her down the hall and into the evidence room. She watched him book in the evidence and make photocopies for her of the bankbook covers and the deposit pages. He stapled them with an itemized receipt on which he listed every detail, names of the banks, the cities and countries, the amounts. She watched him lock the books in the safe with a duplicate of her receipt. The man might be officious, at least sometimes, but he was thorough.

From the police station she drove directly to the Molena Point bank and drew a cashier's check for the forty thousand in their joint savings account. She took that across the street to the Bank of California.

In the cool, high-ceilinged lobby, with its skylights and potted ficus trees, she sat opposite a bank officer at his desk filling out the required cards and forms for an account in her name alone. And, because everyone in Molena Point knew everyone else, she told the young man that she and Jimmie were making some adjustments for tax purposes.

Leaving the bank, she drove north through the village. The sun was pushing up toward noon through a clear blue sky. It was going to be warm, one of those clear sunny innocuous days that, to Californians, sometimes grew tedious by their very bland repetition. Though according to village custom, this kind of grousing was sure to bring on atypical floods, high winds, or earthquake.

She realized she hadn't had breakfast, that she was famished again though she'd stuffed herself so late last night on Clyde's spaghetti and garlic bread. There was a new little restaurant up on Highway One that was supposed to serve light French pancakes, and she headed up Ocean. She'd have breakfast, then drive on up into the hills and sit quietly until time to meet Harper. Take time for a last look at the view she loved; once she was out of town, it might be a long time before she could enjoy the hills again. The morning, despite the sun's brilliance, was still nice and cool. The heat wouldn't descend until afternoon. She drove slowly with her windows down, tasting the salt wind. Going up Ocean she saw patrol cars clustered around the shop, and a shock of coldness hit in her. She pulled over, looking.

The police had blocked off the entry to the shop with two squad cars and some sawhorses, and they had blocked off Haley Street with a patrol car angled across it. An officer stood before the door of the agency showroom, as if to let no one inside. She parked, locked her car, and walked over.

26

The cats crept behind a beam, cringing down as Wark's light swept the attic above them; it returned low, just missed them, flashing over along the top of the heavy timber where they hid.

And suddenly he fired again, into the dark beyond the beam but too close, they heard it ping into the ceiling not three feet from them; it was a wild shot. His light careened on along the base of the slanted roof, searching.

When he failed to find them he fired twice more, wild and uselessly. But he was crawling in their direction, hunching along a narrow joist straight toward them. "Split up," Dulcie whispered. "We can jump him from behind."

"And get blown to confetti."

"Have to make him drop his gun, hit him, and leap away. If he drops it down among those wires, that will give us time while he tries to fish it out."

"I don't think . . . " He had started to say it was a crazy idea, when, from below in the street, sirens screamed.

Nothing, nothing had ever sounded so good.

Immediately Wark's light went out and they heard him scuttle away, back toward the hole in the ceiling. That earsplitting squad car wail was the finest sound Joe had ever imagined.

Two more sirens screamed from the front of the building, then another from the side street. He could just picture the police units careening up Ocean, converging on the agency—fierce and predatory, all muscle.

They sat up and stretched, and slowly their pounding hearts eased into a gentler rhythm. They heard, below, the big metal gates roll open, and then voices. And, nearer, they heard a thud as if Wark had dropped down, perhaps onto the desk in the office.

"Is he gone?" Dulcie breathed.

"He'd better be. This is no way to spend the rest of your life."

"Short lives," she said shakily.

In a moment they heard the smaller gate to the restaurant rattle, then thuds and voices in a confusion of sound, and a shout. Then the whish of the men's room door opening.

When footsteps rang on the tile, they rose and headed for the hole in the ceiling and for civilized company. A click stopped them, a click from the blackness as Wark cocked his revolver. They dropped and crept away; he was still with them.

The ladder rattled, someone was climbing, likely a cop was climbing up. In another second the guy would stick his head up like a target in a shooting gallery. "Look out!" Joe shouted. "He'll shoot! Keep down!"

Joe didn't think about what he was doing. He

had no choice. At his shout, Wark burst out of the blackness half-running, half-crawling. Avoiding the hole into the men's room, he dived for the opening over the office. He was a blur plunging down. They heard him hit the desk, a huge thud, hit the floor, heard him running, and heard a door bang.

They approached the opening and looked over.

The office was empty.

Behind them the ladder clinked again, the rattling of footsteps on the metal rungs.

Joe knew he'd blown it, that the fuzz would be very interested in where that voice came from. Well, so the cops had heard a shout. So there was no human up here. So, what cop was going to believe that was a cat shouting?

Another clink, and another. And Clyde's head appeared rising up through the lit hole.

Joe gaped. He leaped, piling into Clyde, licking his face, purring so hard he choked.

"What the hell? What are you doing up here? What are you so excited about? That was you who shouted! I heard the guy run, heard him jump down." Clyde held him away. "Are you hurt? I don't see any blood. Where's Dulcie?" They heard running and shouting from the laundry, and two more shots were fired somewhere below.

"What the hell's going on, Joe?"

Joe swallowed.

He'd sworn he could never talk face-to-face with Clyde. He stared at Clyde, frozen. He stared until they heard officers' voices ring out from below in the restaurant.

They heard the gate slam again, and a car door slam. Then from behind Joe, a soft voice said, "When are we going to get out of here? I'm tired of this crawl hole. I'm tired of cobwebs on my ears, and I'm tired of being shot at." And Dulcie stolled into the light.

She gave Clyde a green-eyed gaze, and leaped past his face, down through the hole, hitting the ladder twice with quick paws.

Max Harper moved fast into the men's room, and stopped. He studied Clyde, standing on the ladder with his head stuck through the ceiling.

Clyde looked down. "No one up here. Did you get Wark?"

"Picked him up outside the laundry." Harper motioned Clyde down. "Move on out. Who's up there?"

"Not a soul. Just my cat."

"Has to be. I heard someone talking—two voices." He switched off the overhead light, slipped his flashlight from his belt, and started up the ladder.

"There's no one, Max. I was talking to the cats." Clyde backed down the ladder carrying Joe, and glanced across at Dulcie, where she sat demurely out of the way, in the corner. "I don't know how they got in the attic, but they were pretty scared."

"That gray cat's yours? The one I see around the house? I didn't know you brought him to work with you." He scowled at Dulcie. "I don't remember the other one."

Clyde shrugged. "That one belongs to Wilma, I'm cat-sitting." He grinned. "I guess I'm getting old; I talk to them a lot."

From Clyde's shoulder, Joe looked innocently back at Max Harper. He'd spent many a night lying under the kitchen table while Harper and Clyde played poker. Then, Harper usually smelled of horses, but not now, when he was in uniform.

Harper scowled at him, lifted his paw, and looked closely at his claws. Joe looked, too, and saw a trace of blood. Harper said, "Wark's face was torn up pretty bad. Long bloody scratches." He patted Joe, climbed on up the ladder, and shone his light into the darkness, He stood looking for a minute, then climbed up. They could hear him crawling toward the far end.

He made a surprisingly quick survey. He returned, holstered his gun, and swung down the ladder. Then the two men moved out into the restaurant. The cats followed.

The restaurant blazed with light. Every light was on, bouncing against the varnished pine walls, illuminating the stained, flowered carpet.

Harper stood watching his men as they searched, then he grinned at Clyde, the smile making surprising lines in that somber face. "Hey, we have our evidence."

"What, the motor numbers?"

"No. Looks like we have some money deposits. Kate Osborne brought in the bankbooks. They're in the safe, as we speak. Foreign bankbooks, big numbers."

"Well for Pete's sake, all this time . . . Kate didn't tell me about any bankbooks."

Harper shrugged. "She told me."

The four officers searching the room moved nearer to them, and two went behind the bar and began checking the shelves underneath. Joe wasn't sure what they were looking for, but he knew where it had to be hidden. He slipped close to Clyde, and nudged Clyde's ankle with his nose.

Ten minutes later, as Clyde and Max Harper stood in the shop yard, followed closely by Dulcie, an officer shouted to Harper that he had another call on the police radio. Harper stepped over to a squad car to take it, grumbling because the department hadn't been issued cellulars, thanks to local politics.

Joe thought Clyde had handled it very well, just a nudge to the ankle, a flip of the ears toward the door and a long serious look, and Clyde got the message. He had edged on out to the yard, and Harper, finished inside, moved out with him.

When Harper returned, he and Clyde and two officers headed for the men's rest room. Immediately Joe jumped down from beside the bar phone and the other cat followed.

The officers searched the men's room, nearly taking apart the fixtures. They examined the water tank, and two men checked the attic again.

At last Harper said, "That call had to be a hoax. There's not a damn thing in here." He returned to the mirror, and jiggled it, and examined its bracket more closely. Frowning, he wiggled the glass. When it shifted in its frame he attempted to slide it up.

It slid. He lifted it out, revealing a small metal door the size of a medicine cabinet door, set flush into the wall. He leaned the glass against the booth partition.

"Brennan, give me the key you took off Wark."

Brennan handed Harper a brass key. As Harper fitted it into the lock, Joe and Dulcie crowded close between a tangle of uniform trouser legs and black regulation shoes. And though Captain Harper didn't glance down at them, they could tell he was aware of them in that attentive way police had. They hardly breathed as Harper turned the key and opened the metal door.

Crammed inside the little space were four fat plastic bags. Harper pulled them out, opened one, and fanned through a sheaf of hundred dollar bills. Holding one by the edge, he looked at it carefully, then smiled and slipped it back with the rest.

At the back of the rectangular hole was a second metal door. Harper glanced at a thin officer. "Wendell, go check out the laundry, see if you can find this."

Later when the cats were alone, sitting on top of the tow car, their ears assailed by the police radio, and watching two officers fingerprint the Corvette, Dulcie whispered, "I expected it to be drugs in those plastic bags."

"So did I. Who would guess that Wark and Jimmie

were running counterfeit money along with the cars. And laundering the profits from both."

Officer Wendell had found the second door to the medicine cabinet in the laundry office, behind the cubbyholes. After some discussion, a laundry employee had been willing to talk. He told Harper the money was wrapped as laundry, loaded into the delivery trucks, and distributed on the regular route to five other restaurants along with clean uniforms, dinner napkins, and tablecloths. He said that was all he knew.

Police assumed that the money was locked in the cabinet from the men's room side when Wark or Jimmie went for coffee. Harper never did find out who made the anonymous phone call to the station, the call that urged him to search the men's room. The dispatcher said it was a male voice. "Kind of gravelly," she told Harper. "He just said to search the men's room, that it was urgent. Then he hung up."

Joe was still stressed from that call. He'd had to wait while the cops finished searching the front of the restaurant and moved on to the kitchen. As he placed the call from the phone behind the counter, Dulcie followed Harper to be sure he received Joe's message from the dispatcher.

After the money was found, they overheard Captain Harper send two men over to the Osborne house, to pick up Jimmie and Sheril Beckwhite for questioning. Harper kept Lee Wark cuffed in the back of a squad car until they finished up and headed back to the station.

The cats lay stretched out in the sun atop the cab of the tow truck, feeling smug, when Joe glanced up and saw Kate coming from the showroom, walking hesitantly. She stood talking with Clyde and Captain Harper for some time. Then she and Clyde came on across the shop yard. She looked pale. Clyde put his arm around her.

She leaned against his shoulder. "I thought I'd be glad they arrested Jimmie. I don't know how I feel."

She looked at Clyde helplessly. "I gave Harper the evidence to convict my own husband. I'm sending Jimmie to jail." She buried her face against Clyde's shoulder.

Then she moved away, and blew her nose. "Sheril was with him." She started to laugh. "They arrested Sheril." She shook with what Joe thought was pent-up nerves. "The police arrested Jimmie and Sheril . . . " She doubled over, laughing. "Arrested them—in our conjugal bed."

She stopped laughing and clung to Clyde, shivering. "What did I do? What did I do to Jimmie?"

Clyde held her and patted her head.

Joe wanted to say, "Who's sending him to jail. Jimmie's sending himself to jail."

But he hurt for Kate. And he watched her with increasing curiosity, remembering Jimmie's words, the night they followed him in the fog—*Where did the unnatural things come from? How do you think that makes me feel, my own wife . . .*

When at last Kate noticed him, she held out her hand. "Hello, Joe Grey," she said, stroking him. He twisted around, sniffing her fingers, sniffing up her arm. That made her smile. He wanted to tell her she was well rid of Jimmie, that Jimmie Osborne was no good, and that she could do better. He let her pet him and rub his ears until Dulcie growled.

Kate looked startled, and drew her hand back. Joe glared at Dulcie, but Dulcie's dark tabby coat stood straight up, and her tail was huge. Her growl rumbled so fiercely it shook her.

And Kate stopped looking surprised, gave Dulcie a knowing look, and moved away.

But it was not until two nights later, in Jolly's alley, that Dulcie and Kate began to be friends; and that Joe and Dulcie were put to the final terrifying test of their strange metamorphosis.

27

Old Mr. Jolly, coming out to the softly lit alley to deposit his garbage before he closed up for the night, and to leave a nice plate of scraps for the village cats, paused, puzzled.

The alley was empty, yet just as he stepped out he had heard laughter. It had seemed to be right outside the door.

There was no one passing on the well-lit street. He stepped to the street and looked both ways, but there was no one on this block. Maybe his hearing was going bad, playing tricks.

The only occupants of the alley were two cats, prancing across the bricks batting a leaf back and forth, chasing it through the glow of the wall lamps. Jolly put down his plate of scraps beside the jasmine vine and stood watching them, amused by their antics.

He guessed they weren't very hungry. Certainly they could smell the good veal and ham, but they didn't rush to the plate. He knew these two, and they weren't shy about tying into a nice snack. Both were eager guests at his feline buffet. The little

brown tabby belonged to Wilma Getz, who worked
in the reference department of the library. He
watched the tabby roll over coyly on the brick,
glancing sideways at the tom as she reached to bat
the leaf. What a flirt; her green eyes were dancing.
She seemed as happy as if she owned the world. So
maybe she did own it, who knew about cats? The
gray tom circled her, feinting at the leaf, then leaped
at her and they scuffled. Jolly laughed; it pleased
him to see animals so filled with joy, so happy with
being alive.

The cats played for a few minutes, then sat
regarding him. And at last they trotted on over,
looked up at him bright-eyed and smiling, and tied
into the scraps of warm veal roll and the hickory-
smoked ham and the crab salad. He liked the way
cats enjoyed their food. The tom smacked and gob-
bled, but the little tabby ate delicately. Interesting
that the tom, though he was bigger, shared equally
with the tabby, leaving half for her.

The tidbits he set out were never large, but when
they were arranged all together onto a paper plate
they made a respectable meal. He found it curious
that people left good food on their plates. It was
never the fat folks—they cleaned up every bite. It
was the thin women, the ones who looked like they
needed a little nourishment. They left the nicest
scraps.

As the two cats feasted, a third cat appeared out
of the dark vines at the end of the alley. As it paused
beneath the light, its creamy color shone bright, and
its eyes gleamed golden. This was a new cat; Jolly

did not know this one. It had to be a female, so round and sweet-faced, such a pretty cat. As she drew closer he could see that her cream-colored fur was streaked with orange, like rich whipped cream folded with a dash of apricot jam.

She might be a stranger, but she trotted right on down the alley bold as you please, toward the scrap plate. She stopped once to rub her shoulder against the container of a potted tree, obliquely observing the two cats as if assessing them. The two feasting cats watched her indirectly, their ears twisting toward her, but they did not stop eating.

The cream cat was bold as brass—she trotted right up to the plate, pushed the gray tom aside, and took what was left of his share. The tom didn't object, but the tabby cat lashed her tail, laid back her ears, screamed, and lit into the cream cat, biting and clawing. Jolly didn't know whether to stop her or let them alone.

Before he could make up his mind, the scuffle was finished. The two backed off glaring at each other and then looked at the tom. And something strange happened.

The two females, without any more preliminaries, suddenly seemed to make friends. They approached each other with their ears and whiskers forward in a friendly way, sat down near one another, and began to wash their paws. The tom stood looking on, seeming as amused by them as Jolly felt.

Cats. Who knew what went on in those furry little heads.

He picked up the empty paper plate, dropped it in the garbage, and went back inside, leaving the night to the cats, to those amazing beasts.

When Jolly had gone, the three cats trotted away up the alley side by side and disappeared into the dark shadows beneath the jasmine vine.

There, sheltered by tangles of small, dense leaves dotted with yellow blossoms, the cream cat lay down and washed herself more thoroughly. She did not speak for some time. She looked Dulcie and Joe over, her face registering a dozen expressions. They looked back uneasily, and Dulcie shivered. She was both afraid of what would happen, and excited. Joe regarded the cream cat with puzzled unease, and he had to keep reminding himself that this was Kate. This was Kate Osborne.

Kate wasn't one to make small talk. When she spoke, it was in strange, rhyming words. Words that clung like honey in the cats' minds. At the rich sounds a tingling dizziness filled Joe. The shadows tilted. He thought he was falling, he clawed at the foliage to steady himself.

But soon his dizziness was gone. Nothing more happened. He crouched in alarm, his stub tail tucked down, his ears flat.

He hadn't liked the feeling of being out of control, of being pulled away from himself. For a minute he'd felt like some vaporized sci-fi hero zapped away into another dimension.

If that was part of the program, he'd pass, thank

you. He glanced at Dulcie. She, too, had remained herself. She did not look happy.

Dulcie had felt nothing at all. She could have gotten a better buzz from a sprig of catnip.

The cream cat tried again, repeating the bright rhyme, but still nothing happened. Joe and Dulcie remained small and four-footed.

The cream cat's eyes narrow, puzzled, then widened. Standing within the thick shadows, she said the words a third time and this time she allowed herself to change. She was suddenly tall, her hair tangled in the vine, her blouse caught on the twigs.

The cats stared up at her. Dulcie's green eyes were huge with envy.

Kate said, "Did you feel nothing?"

Joe felt relief. He had no desire to do that stuff. One try was more than he wanted. He was a cat— he had everything he needed just as he was. His human thoughts, his human talents, his ability to read and speak, worked just fine in his own gray fur. He had the best of both worlds. He was Joe Grey, enjoying his human talents without human entanglements. Free and unencumbered.

But Dulcie was crushed. When she realized she couldn't change, she had crouched, desolate, her ears down, her tail tucked under.

Joe nuzzled her and licked her face, but she couldn't respond.

Ever since the day in the automotive yard when she saw, within Kate's eyes, a cat looking back at her, when she saw the astonishing truth of what was possible, she had allowed herself magnificent dreams.

Visions of becoming tall and dark-haired and beautiful, visions of her green-eyed human self, had driven and excited her. She had imagined going out to fancy restaurants, attending the symphony and plays, had dreamed of dancing, of slipping into silk cocktail dresses and spike heels, into little satin bras and lace panties. "Try again," she whispered.

Kate tried. Dulcie tried with her, repeating the words as Kate said them. But it was no use. Dulcie remained a cat. A tear slid down her fur, a human tear.

Kate knelt in the shadows beside her, touching Dulcie's face. "There could be other spells. Maybe another spell . . . "

"Maybe," Dulcie said, not believing it. "Maybe . . . "

But then she looked at Joe. Cocking her head, she saw for the first time how relieved he was. She'd been too busy with her own disappointment to see him brighten when Kate's words didn't work. She reached to lick his nose. "Why?" she said, pressing close to him. "Why don't you want to change?"

He nibbled an itch on his paw, and gave her a long, unblinking look. "We're like nothing else, Dulcie. You and I and Kate—and maybe a few others somewhere. We are unique."

"So?" She waited, puzzled.

"I want to enjoy what I have. Don't you see? I like the change just as it is. I've been having a ball." His eyes were bright, intense. "I liked being a special cat. I like being a *cat*. I like my new skills, but most of all I like what I am."

She tried to understand. He was aware, sentient, yet totally feline. And he was perfectly happy.

She was quiet for a long time.

At last she touched Kate's hand with her paw. "No more spells," she said softly. And she pressed against Joe, purring. If Joe was content, then maybe she would be, too. Maybe this was the better way. She would try his way, and see how she felt about it. Try enjoying this new life just as she was—while she went on stealing silk teddies.

28

Once a year Jolly's Deli held a party in the alley. George Jolly and his staff set up tables and chairs along the brick lane, and out along the sidewalk, and served an elegant cold buffet of their specialty salads, cold roast turkey and pastrami and roast beef, and assorted cheeses and breads and desserts. The annual affair was a big event in Molena Point, a time for neighbors to get together. Even the village cats could party if they cared to brave the noisy crowd. George Jolly himself arranged leftovers for the cats on a row of paper plates beside the back door.

This year, so soon after Samuel Beckwhite's murder, many villagers assumed that Jolly would postpone or cancel the event, but he did not. What better way to dispel the ugly memories of what had occurred in the alley than to fill the lane with good cheer and comradery.

Though the case was not yet closed, though portions of the investigation were still under way, the shock and overwrought publicity had subsided, and the Molena Point Gazette had relegated any new developments to the third page.

Lee Wark had been booked for murder, for grand theft auto, and for passing counterfeit bills. Jimmie Osborne's charges were similar, but he was booked as an accomplice to the murder of Samuel Beckwhite.

The murder weapon, a British-made torque wrench, had turned up on the seat of a patrol car which had been left unlocked for a moment in the station parking lot. The weapon was wrapped in a plastic bag. The plastic had been buried; it was stained with garden soil. The police lab identified the dirt as coming from a garden that grew marigolds. That could be half the gardens in Molena Point. The lab was trying to pinpoint the exact location of the garden, but that would take some time. They did find on the wrench traces of Beckwhite's blood. And they found Lee Wark's prints superimposed over Clyde Damen's prints. Damen had identified the wrench as among the tools stolen shortly before the murder, from his automotive repair shop.

A pair of thin rubber gloves was found in Wark's car, and sent to the lab. Captain Harper said that it wasn't uncommon for fingerprints to go right through the thin, surgical rubber. Wark's prints, plus testimony by the woman who had been in the alley the night of the murder, would be enough to indict the Welshman for Beckwhite's death. The witness saw Wark hit Beckwhite and she saw Beckwhite fall.

"And it wasn't a man, after all," Joe said.

Dulcie widened her eyes. "How could I tell it was a woman, in the pitch-dark? I couldn't smell her, my nose was so full of the scent of jasmine I couldn't have smelled a rotting fish."

But even with the weapon and the killer's prints accounted for, the investigation was not complete. Evidence led police to believe that Beckwhite had been a knowing accomplice in the sale of stolen cars, and that matter was still under scrutiny. Sheril Beckwhite swore to police that her husband didn't know about the counterfeit money, nor did she. Sheril had been indicted as an accomplice to the theft of the cars, but not as an accomplice in her husband's murder. That, too, was still under investigation. The common assumption around the village was that, even if she was convicted for car theft, Sheril would get probation.

Beckwhite's funeral had been an impressive occasion. He had been put to rest with mountains of flowers and an endless parade of mourners. The funeral entourage, which ran heavily to gleaming foreign cars, was so long that for two hours the entire village had to be cordoned off by the police, effectively preventing entry into Molena Point even from Highway One.

But once Samuel Beckwhite was laid to rest in the prestigious St. Mark's Cemetery, which occupied a high hillside plateau above Molena Point Valley, George Jolly set about planning his annual party. He announced the date, as he always did, by taking out a half-page ad in the *Gazette*. The party was planned for just seven weeks after the arrest of Lee Wark and Jimmie Osborne.

Arrested, as well, and out on bond were the owners

of Mom's Burgers and of the adjoining laundry, for
trafficking in counterfeit bills. Max Harper still had
no idea who his informant was, who had given him
the location of the money, and had anonymously
turned over the murder weapon. He had questioned
all employees of Mom's Burgers, of the laundry, of
the automotive agency. The phone call which
relayed to him the location of the counterfeit bills
behind the mirror in the men's room had alerted
him, as well, that the VIN number on the yellow
Corvette had been changed. The dispatcher had pru-
dently made a tape of the voice. Everyone in the
department had listened. No one recognized it.

Bernine Sage, the agency bookkeeper, had not
come forward with her eyewitness account of the
murder until Wark and Osborne had been arrested,
claiming she was afraid to do so until they were
behind bars. She had described the killing accurate-
ly, and had shown Harper where she was standing,
concealed behind the combined shelter of the jasmine bush and the oleander tree when Wark killed
Beckwhite. She said she had been headed for the
drugstore that night, looking in the gallery windows
when she came abreast of the alley and heard low
voices. She had glanced in at the precise moment
that Wark hit Beckwhite.

The day of the party was bright and cool with
very little breeze. The two dozen long tables occupied not only the alley but the sidewalks on both
streets. They had been covered with white paper
tablecloths, as were the two long buffet tables which
dominated the alley itself. These were loaded with

an array of Jolly's most popular delicacies. Coffee and soft drinks were served by Jolly's staff, four young men dressed in their usual immaculate white uniforms.

Captain Harper, standing in line at the buffet, was deeply preoccupied with the several puzzling loose ends to the Beckwhite case. For in spite of his unanswered questions, the case was wrapping up neatly. Two and a quarter million in counterfeit bills. Six restaurant owners already indicated for passing counterfeit money. And his department was slowly putting together a complete picture of the money laundering operation which spread to the East Coast and the Caribbean.

He heaped his plate with Jolly's delicacies and headed down the alley to Clyde's table, where Clyde had saved him a chair. Sitting down next to Wilma, he was amused that Clyde and Wilma had brought their two cats. The cats were sitting on a chair right at the table, sitting side by side, very straight, looking around as if they were enjoying themselves. A well-trained dog might do that, but cats?

Max wasn't a cat person; he much preferred the more direct friendship of dogs and horses. But he had to admire the skill of anyone who could get a pair of cats to sit quietly at the table in a crowded environment. In his experience, cats were skittery and easily frightened. He glanced up to where old Jolly was watching from his doorway, and old Jolly was looking at the cats, too. George Jolly was a real cat nut, worse than Clyde, always feeding the animals. There was always a plate in the alley, always cats hanging around.

Watching the two cats at the table, Max thought about these cats the morning of the arrests up at Mom's Burgers. He could see again the two cats standing right there among his officers watching intently as he removed the mirror and unlocked the metal door. When he lifted out the bags of counterfeit bills they had stared, had seemed almost excited.

He knew he was obsessed with cats. But the whole case seemed tainted by cats—that joke at the station about a cat walking through as if it owned the place, that had happened the morning Clyde brought him the list of stolen cars. And the night of Beckwhite's murder, there'd been a cat; some cat had run out from the alley. The patrol field sheet noted that a cat fled from the alley into the car's lights at about the time Beckwhite had been killed.

He watched Kate serve a small paper plate from her own plate, glancing down at the two cats. So Kate was another one—a big cat person.

Kate was doing very well, he thought, considering the last few weeks. She seemed to be shaking off the failed marriage and becoming eager to get on with her life. He'd heard she had put her house on the market and was talking about moving up to San Francisco for a while. Be good for her. Change of scene, new interests.

He watched her set the small plate down on the chair, watched the cats bend eagerly to the salmon salad and bits of cold meats. But the cats were far too mannerly; their unnatural behavior increased his unease. And when Clyde asked the gray tomcat if he wanted more roast beef, and the cat mewled stridently, Harper's blood chilled.

He hardly attended as Wilma said, "I'm glad to have Dulcie home, I missed her." She was speaking to Clyde, but she seemed almost to be speaking to the cat. "I bought her a new silk pillow, and a little Dresden supper bowl, after I cracked hers with my shovel.

"I thought I'd start taking her to the library, it's quite the thing among libraries now, to have a resident cat. I think she'd like to do that. A good many librarians say that a library cat has increased their book circulation."

Harper had known Wilma a long time, he knew when she was putting him on. He grinned and winked at her.

But she looked back at him dead serious. "It's true, Max. Cats do increase library traffic, children and old people particularly will come in to pet the cat, and will stay to do a little browsing, end up with a stack of books. And cats are wonderful at story hour, a loving little cat can calm the children, and keep them from fidgeting. There's even a Library Cat Society. I think Dulcie will fit right in. I think she'll find the experience—entertaining."

Max patted Wilma's hand. "I'm sure she will," he said, trying to imagine the city fathers allowing a cat in the library. He guessed Wilma was getting a bit dotty. He didn't understand the sense of strangeness that gripped him. After all, Wilma was just another cat nut.

He finished his coffee and rose. He needed to get back to the station. Needed to ease down into the normal confusion of routine police work, shake off the weirdness.

But on his way out of the alley, when he turned to look back, both cats were watching him. He could swear they were laughing.

Murder Is on the Menu
at the Hillside Manor Inn
Bed-and-Breakfast Mysteries by
MARY DAHEIM
featuring Judith McMonigle Flynn

CREEPS SUZETTE 0-380-80079-9/ $6.50 US/ $8.99 Can

BANTAM OF THE OPERA
0-380-76934-4/ $6.50 US/ $8.99 Can

JUST DESSERTS 0-380-76295-1/ $6.99 US/ $9.99 Can

FOWL PREY 0-380-76296-X/ $6.99 US/ $9.99 Can

HOLY TERRORS 0-380-76297-8/ $6.99 US/ $9.99 Can

DUNE TO DEATH 0-380-76933-6/ $6.50 US/ $8.50 Can

A FIT OF TEMPERA 0-380-77490-9/ $6.99 US/ $9.99 Can

MAJOR VICES 0-380-77491-7/ $6.50 US/ $8.99 Can

MURDER, MY SUITE 0-380-77877-7/ $6.50 US/ $8.99 Can

AUNTIE MAYHEM 0-380-77878-5/ $6.50 US/ $8.50 Can

NUTTY AS A FRUITCAKE
0-380-77879-3/ $6.50 US/ $8.99 Can

SEPTEMBER MOURN 0-380-78518-8/ $6.50 US/ $8.99 Can

WED AND BURIED 0-380-78520-X/ $6.50 US/ $8.99 Can

SNOW PLACE TO DIE 0-380-78521-8/ $6.99 US/ $9.99 Can

LEGS BENEDICT 0-380-80078-0/ $6.50 US/ $8.50 Can

A STREETCAR NAMED EXPIRE
0-380-80080-2/ $6.99 US/ $9.99 Can

SUTURE SELF
0-380-81561-3/$6.99 US/ $9.99 Can

And in Hardcover

SILVER SCREAM
0-380-97867-9/ $23.95 US/ $36.50 Can

JILL CHURCHILL

Delightful Mysteries Featuring
Suburban Mom Jane Jeffry

THE HOUSE OF SEVEN MABELS
0-380-97736-2/$23.95 US/$36.50 CAN

GRIME AND PUNISHMENT
0-380-76400-8/$6.99 US/$9.99 CAN

A FAREWELL TO YARNS 0-380-76399-0/$6.99 US/$9.99 CAN

A QUICHE BEFORE DYING
0-380-76932-8/$6.99 US/$9.99 CAN

THE CLASS MENAGERIE 0-380-77380-5/$6.50 US/$8.99 CAN

A KNIFE TO REMEMBER 0-380-77381-3/$5.99 US/$7.99 CAN

FROM HERE TO PATERNITY
0-380-77715-0/$6.99 US/$9.99 CAN

SILENCE OF THE HAMS 0-380-77716-9/$6.99 US/$9.99 CAN

WAR AND PEAS 0-380-78706-7/$6.99 US/$9.99 CAN

FEAR OF FRYING 0-380-78707-5/$5.99 US/$7.99 CAN

THE MERCHANT OF MENACE
0-380-79449-7/$6.99 US/$9.99 CAN

A GROOM WITH A VIEW 0-380-79450-0/$6.50 US/$8.99 CAN

MULCH ADO ABOUT NOTHING
0-380-80491-3/$6.50 US/$8.99 CAN

The Grace & Favor Mysteries

ANYTHING GOES 0-380-80244-9/$6.99 US/$9.99 CAN

IN THE STILL OF THE NIGHT
0-380-80245-7/$6.99 US/$9.99 CAN

SOMEONE TO WATCH OVER ME
0-06-103123-2/$6.99 US/$9.99 CAN

DEN OF ANTIQUITY MYSTERIES

by
TAMAR MYERS

LARCENY AND OLD LACE
0-380-78239-1/$5.99 US/$7.99 Can

GILT BY ASSOCIATION
0-380-78237-5/$6.50 US/$8.50 Can

THE MING AND I
0-380-79255-9/$6.50 US/$8.99 Can

SO FAUX, SO GOOD
0-380-79254-0/$6.50 US/$8.99 Can

BAROQUE AND DESPERATE
0-380-80225-2/$6.50 US/$8.99 Can

ESTATE OF MIND
0-380-80227-9/$6.50 US/$8.99 Can

A PENNY URNED
0-380-81189-8/$6.50 US/$8.99 Can

NIGHTMARE IN SHINING ARMOR
0-380-81191-X/$6.50 US/$8.99 Can

SPLENDOR IN THE GLASS
0-380-81964-3/$6.99 US/$9.99 Can

Discover Murder and Mayhem with

Southern Sisters Mysteries
by
ANNE GEORGE

MURDER ON A GIRLS' NIGHT OUT
0-380-78086-0/$6.99 US/$9.99 Can
Agatha Award winner for Best First Mystery Novel

MURDER ON A BAD HAIR DAY
0-380-78087-9/$6.99 US/$9.99 Can

MURDER RUNS IN THE FAMILY
0-380-78449-1/$6.99 US/$9.99 Can

MURDER MAKES WAVES
0-380-78450-5/$6.99 US/$9.99 Can

MURDER GETS A LIFE
0-380-79366-0/$6.99 US/$9.99 Can

MURDER SHOOTS THE BULL
0-380-80149-3/$6.99 US/$9.99 Can

MURDER CARRIES A TORCH
0-380-80938-9/$6.99 US/$9.99 Can

MURDER BOOGIES WITH ELVIS
0-06-103102-X/$6.99 US/$9.99 Can